I0799833

Fables Obscura

Red Rook Press

This is a work of fiction. Any references to actual persons, living or dead, events, or locales are used fictitiously

To request permissions, contact the publisher at redrookpress@gmail.com.

Paperback: 979-8-9879562-9-8
Ebook: 979-8-9929709-0-6

First paperback edition April 2025

Cover design: DeAndra Gauntt

artwork: Anna Cobb, MiKayla Davis, Alexandria Gauntt, DeAndra Gauntt, Elizabeth Golembiewski, Andrew Kelley, Anna Luis, Anna White

Printed by Mixam in the United States of America.

Red Rook Press
Box 870244
The University of Alabama
Tuscaloosa, AL 35487-0244

redrookpress.org

Fables Obscura

stories

Peter Prizel

Stories

for Sam

Newton's Rainbow

The sun struggled to break free from the gray skies, whose vapor-laden clouds hung over the campus of Trinity College in Cambridge, as Sir Isaac took stock of his life. It had been forty years since he had proven that clear white light was comprised of seven colors, and eighteen since he had formulated his theory of gravity, and now he was finally knighted. After fixing his new coat of arms, two white tibiae set in the shape of an X against black background on a shield, to the window of his study, the esteemed physicist set to work polishing the prism with which he had conducted his light experiments.

Sir Isaac hoped the day would have been sunny so that he could resummon the rainbow which had demonstrated that seven colors are visible in clear white light. He had hoped that his striped friend would join him. Like the apple that had fallen on his head—whereby Newton postulated his theory of gravity—Newton's work on light and color were among his most important discoveries. In fact, these two discoveries of colors and gravity led Queen Anne to knight him. It was this occasion of knighthood that Sir Isaac was hoping to celebrate with the rainbow.

"You have stayed there faithfully in that little corner of yours," Newton said to the apple, which rested on its own specially-designated oak table in one corner of his study. He opened the curtain to his window only to see that it was still cloudy. "If only the weather would cooperate, then our honorable friend Rainbow could join us. Why, I even purchased a double malt whiskey from Scotland for the occasion! But no matter, I will busy myself by answering some letters until the sun comes out."

The scientist hobbled over to his desk set against the corner of his dank study, lit a candle, and read the correspondence that had just arrived. "South Sea Company shares plummet and lose half value" read the headline of the newspaper clipping that accompanied a letter from the banker who managed Newton's funds.

"Bastards would have been better off drowning," Newton muttered. "Had they, I could have at least collected some insurance money." Newton did not even take the time to read the equations on the small index card that accompanied the letter denoting he had just lost some £20,000. Rays of the sun began to show through the partially-drawn satin curtain, which covered the window overlooking the courtyard of the university.

"Ah!" Sir Isaac exclaimed with pleasure. "Now Rainbow can make himself known!" He closed the shutter and held the prism up against a small hole so that he could refract the sunbeam onto the far wall of his study. The day was not as sunny as it had been forty years ago, and it took Newton a few maneuvers to line up his prism with the ray of light. Amid curses and shouts, Newton finally got the shaft of light to cooperate. Within a quarter of an hour, he had the colors red, orange, yellow, green, blue, indigo, and violet refracting directly over the unfortunate correspondence he had just received.

"I had thought that you would summon me today," Rainbow said when he was fully established against the wall. "It is our fortieth anniversary."

"I would have indeed, but I have requested your presence for an additional reason," Newton began.

"If you want my opinion about your financial losses, I fear I am going to overstay my welcome," Rainbow replied.

"Surely, you will have a drink with me, and then, if I am in a merrier mood, we can consider discussing what happened on the high seas," Newton said as he poured himself and Rainbow each a shot of whiskey.

"But of course," Rainbow said. "I could not help but notice on my way in that you hung up a coat of arms. I take it that you are moving up in the world."

"Indeed," Newton replied. "I have been knighted, finally."

"You have risen to the peerage," Rainbow told the physicist.

"At last," Newton said. "And I believe it is no accident that it occurred on our fortieth anniversary."

"If that was the Queen's intention, it would be very fortuitous," Rainbow replied. "But tell me about the motives behind your choice in a coat of arms. Why white crossbones against a pitch-black background?"

"Why, to show my authority. It is common knowledge that crossbones were first seen on the tomb of Tutankhamen in Egypt where he is holding the flail and the crook to denote *his* authority. Just look how I have made sense of darkness, grasped reason out of it, if you will."

"Ah, so my surmising that heraldry as a mea culpa of sorts is a mistake," Rainbow said.

"I thought you did not want to overstay your welcome. Isn't that what you just told me before I poured you a drink?" Newton asked his captive as he picked up his glass from the table and refilled it, nudging the prism with his signet ring so that the violet light's width was cut in third.

"I did not intend to. I was just so sure of myself," Rainbow replied.

"Well, since you have let the cat out of the bag, let's hear your theory," Newton said. "Besides, my mind needs a conundrum to work with so it does not dwell on the huge loss I have just endured."

"One could say that I read your coat of arms at the other end of the spectrum," Rainbow began. "I am a product of white light, a product of physics. To the physicist, white is not a color, but to artists it is, along with black. After glancing down at your ledger and seeing where your losses stem from, I was under the impression that your twisted cross, the hallmark of a scientist who places logic above faith, on a black background was your way of letting all of Cambridge know how indebted your discoveries and the ability to finance them are because of the very human beings South Sea Company trades in."

"I am glad you think so highly of my conscience," Newton commented as he chewed on a fingernail on his left hand, pushing the prism with his right to completely obscure the violet coming from the white light he had created in his study. "Tell me, would you be thinking this way if you were on the other end of the spectrum, say you were not white light but white paint?"

"Who knows, but would your soul rest easier if black was not considered a color? If say you lived in the time of the Greeks and Romans when humanity enslaved one another not on the basis of race?"

"Perhaps," Newton replied as he shifted the prism yet again to make the indigo appear lighter. "But I can't imagine you feel that good either, enslaving all those other colors under you."

"I don't control the weather or the prism in your hand," Rainbow retorted.

"Is there a pot of gold at your other end? Perhaps if you can reimburse me for my losses we can finish this conversation in a civilized manner," Newton said, angling the prism so that the indigo was now out of sight.

"I don't know, as I am not my own master, which you are so clearly demonstrating," Rainbow said.

"Neither was he." Newton gestured to the apple on the oak table. "Had he not happened upon a gust of wind he would not have fallen and ended up on my desk."

"Ah, but he," Rainbow said, pointing to the apple, "he is the symbol of free will, straight out of the Garden of Eden. How you cultivate that free will is up to you, but I hope you do so in such a way that your sense of humanity grows."

"The timing of this letter and pontificating to me about its deeper meaning, along with free will, makes my situation very grave," Newton conceded.

"I am glad you realize its gravity," Rainbow said.

"That was not an invitation for you to speak," Newton said, as he cut the blue from his line of sight. "Perhaps I should repaint my coat of arms. Perhaps I should have two black tibiae in the foreground against a white background."

"And have the color trapped in a sea of void?" Rainbow exclaimed. "Why, unless you intend to divest entirely from the South Sea Company, such blazonry will smack of eugenics."

"Really," Newton mused. "I had actually thought of such an exercise as masochistic on my part."

"Again, it would only be that if you divest in the South Sea Company."

"I am seriously considering it given how much money I lost," Newton huffed as he restricted the view of his guest even more so that only the colors red, orange, and yellow were visible on the wall.

"I can tell you that your coat of arms is certainly relevant when it comes to me," Rainbow said defiantly. "That prism of yours, why it is both a flail and a crook."

"Yes, and if you keep singing the same tune that you have for the past fifteen minutes, it will continue to be the former," Sir Isaac said. He poured himself another glass of whiskey and picked up the apple from its oak table and began to polish it on his sleeve.

"Then thanks be to God that I exist in nature—" Rainbow began only to be cut short by a clap of thunder.

"Perhaps your natural counterpart is at hand," Newton said as he shut down the yellow from his vision. "I honestly did not envision celebrating my knighthood this way. If only this letter had reached me even a day later. Or better yet, if only the rain had started earlier today."

"Will I be invited back for the next grand occasion in your life?" Rainbow inquired.

"That depends on how you behave," Sir Isaac replied. "I cannot imagine that you intended our anniversary to go down this road either."

"Certainly not," Rainbow said. "I did anticipate being summoned today, but I did not expect to discuss such matters. Had the letter not come, we would probably be on our third glass of scotch right now."

"Do you really think I am so rotten to the core?" Newton asked and took a bite from his renowned apple. Rainbow looked away in horror.

"I think the theory that one race is above others is," Rainbow replied. "Until you see black as a color, until you see black human beings as being on par with your own, until you approach other lives from the vantage point of a caring artist and not a cold, removed physicist, I will think of you as rotten."

"Ah, theories, that is all they are. They can never be proven. They can only be tested again and again so that there is more empirical data to back them up, and thereby more subscribers," Newton said.

"Yes, but they are supposed to be to the benefit of mankind, or in theory they are," Rainbow replied.

"And, if we could agree on a hypothesis, the theory in question would be to mankind's benefit. If you want to continue drinking with me, are you willing to continue discussing color from the perspective of a physicist and not that of an artist?" Newton asked his guest, making the orange light invisible and daring Rainbow to challenge him and his trade in fellow human beings.

"The highest art form is change and sometimes change is hard," Rainbow said. "In your ivory tower, no one will know that your coat of arms is really a Jolly Roger that preys on innocent souls. I just hope that even if your head does not reach a different conclusion your heart one day does. I—"

"I am a scientist, and I pray before that alter alone!" Newton bellowed as he cut the Rainbow and decapitated the red light. The physicist then downed a fourth shot of scotch as the thunder receded. After resting for a few minutes, he drew the curtains to his study only to see that his guest had just been banished across the sky.

"I can see that you have made yourself welcome in nature, but soon you will be gone from there. You can only last for a brief time after a rainstorm!" The physicist scoffed and shook his fist at Rainbow while eating the other half of his apple. After spitting out the seeds, Newton cursed and then muttered to the famous apple resting in his hand, "Let's test this theory out again. Go and see if there is a pot of gold at Rainbow's other end. If there really is one, if such talk is not legend, come back to me, and then I will consider divesting from South Sea."

Lightning Over Boston

Ever since the kite had been given life by Benjamin Franklin, the Founding Father's co-discoverer of harnessing electricity had been an ardent deist, professing this ideology not only because his late master had but also because he was disgusted by what he saw. After being passed down to Franklin's children, then sold to an enterprising businessman in Boston, the kite realized that all the churches he flew over, the tallest buildings in every colonial American city, were just a repository of God's ego.

The kite had developed these feelings about churches as he watched the congregants still offer their praises to The Almighty even after lightning and thunderstorms, caused by Him, struck and damaged the houses of worship, as well as other buildings in their vicinity. To the kite, such behaviors by churchgoers made no sense; he saw their praying as futile attempts to placate a vengeful god. Such beliefs were irrational, and they flew in the face of his deist beliefs that God's existence could only be explained by rational thought. Our kite could not understand why people who believed that storms and lightning were symbols of divine retribution would continue to scratch God behind the ears with their praises like a cat sitting in the lap of an old widow who had no one else to console her in her later years.

It was with this mentality that our kite entered the tavern on Boston's north end near Paul Revere's House. The unicorn and lion, who had once graced the Old State house of Boston until the revolution, had lived clandestinely in British sympathizers' houses, venturing out on a night or two for a drink when the townspeople were asleep. Tonight was one of those nights.

"I received your letter and came as fast as I could." The kite doffed his hat when he found the married couple in the back of the saloon by the fireplace.

"Sit down, sit down," the lion said, rising to pull out a chair for the kite. "I am glad you could make it. I know you are wondering why my wife and I have requested your presence. Although our politics differ, I assure you we will make your visit worth your while."

The kite half listened as he cast a sideways glance at the unicorn. With her long silky mane, radiant blue eyes, horn around which ran a spiral of perfect proportions that only the most skilled woodcarvers could imitate, and her smooth white coat, she was a sight to behold.

"I don't know if you read the paper this morning," the lion said as he took a puff of a cigar, "but they are planning to tear down the Old South Meeting House and rebuild it with brick. The citizens fear a fire like the one that struck a church in New York about six months ago."

"I did not hear this, but I am aware of the fire that ravaged New York," the kite said.

"Well, this is what they intend to do, those crazy religious fanatics," the lion continued. "We have been itching for revenge, and my wife and I managed to smuggle in some of these." The lion reached under the table and pulled out a long wooden chest that resembled one that was used at The Boston Tea Party forty years ago. The keyhole was an odd shape, and the kite wondered what kind of key could open it. His question was soon answered when the unicorn inserted her horn into the hole and made a ninety-degree turn. The chest popped open to reveal scores of lightning rods with round tips at the end.

"I trust you are familiar with these," the lion said.

"Of course, I am," the kite said. "Why, they are my de facto children, invented by Franklin as an offshoot of his discovery of electricity."

"Indeed. And are you aware that lightning rods with pointy tips are less likely to be struck than ones with knobs when they are of equal height? Electricity will strike a knobby one because of the greater area."

"Yes, I am. I also recall Franklin grinning with delight when he read about the fires in London as revenge for King George III forbidding his pointy colonial ones to be employed there. Many of the buildings that caught fire in Britain did so only because they were not well grounded, and their going up in flames had nothing to do with knobby English rods. Even so, Franklin took their destruction as a license to say the pointy ones that he invented were superior to those being used across the Atlantic."

"Yes, indeed. King George forbade any American pointy rods installed in England. His hatred for the colonies was so great that he assumed that even a life-saving invention originating from them was suspect. This conversation is not about what King George would approve of or not, or that I am Tory, and you are an American. My wife and I are asking you to fly up to the roof of the Old South Meeting House and install our British knobby rods. Per *The Farmer's Almanac*, it is supposed to rain heavily next week, and we are hoping for a storm. With your installation of the rods, hopefully lightning will strike the Meeting House that doubles as a church for Puritans, causing it to catch fire and burn to the ground. I know how much you hate religious houses that stroke God's ego and why I have urged you to pay us a visit."

The kite reached for a cigar and glided to the fireplace where he lit it in the dying embers, not drawing attention from the innkeeper who was polishing glasses. The kite took a long draw, exhaled, blew a plume and said, "It is true that I hate seeing its citizens duped by religious fanaticism. But you are asking me to betray my country that I love. If the Meeting House burns down, won't they build one of brick, anyway? And then, when fires are no longer an issue, will they act more rationally in their thoughts about God as a vengeful being?"

"Who knows," the unicorn said, "but you must judge whether your hatred for Bostonians' puritanical ways is greater than what the future may or may not hold. My husband and I have always been true to our ideals. We love and have always loved the monarchy and believe we are on British soil. Even when America won independence, we did not leave, nor do we intend to leave now."

The kite looked at the unicorn and almost blushed. He was so smitten by her that his heart skipped a beat. She was so beautiful. He had to spend more time with her even if it meant committing treason.

"Let me think about your proposal," the kite replied as he doffed his hat. "I will let you know by the end of the week." And he took his leave.

The tavern was the worst venue the couple could have chosen to meet the kite, not realizing it was run by one of Paul Revere's assistants who worked nights after apprenticing as a silversmith to the great patriot by day.

Before the sun had risen, the apprentice had informed Revere of what he had heard.

"One if by land, and two if by sea, and on the opposite shore we will be," Revere mused, reciting the famous poem about him. "Longfellow's poem that immortalizes me only recounts my lighting one lantern if the British come by land and two if they come by sea."

"Well, perhaps a line about the sky should be added," the apprentice quipped. "What are we to do? The lion and the unicorn, the jilted Tories, intend to burn down the Meeting House and use that kite as an accomplice."

"Keep your eyes on that British couple and the kite," Revere said. "And let me know immediately what they are up to."

The apprentice began his watch and soon found himself indirectly wrapped up in the conspirators' scheme. The day after the kite had visited the tavern, he ordered a drink, and while under the influence of alcohol, confessed his love for the unicorn.

"I have written these letters to her," the kite said to the apprentice after he downed another Sam Adams. "If only I could find a way to send them to her. Her husband must not see me deliver them."

"Perhaps I can be of help," the apprentice offered, eager to be in the kite's good graces as he gathered information about their plot.

"Thank you, I'd be much obliged," the kite said.

Within a day of the kite's visit to the tavern, the apprentice was passing letters clandestinely to the unicorn. Soon, the letters were going in both directions, the unicorn bribing the apprentice to buy her ink and parchment so she could pen her letters to the kite. With the kite and the unicorn discovering their affection for each other, and the apprentice loaning out his loft above the bar, the lovers could carry on their amorous affair in the wee hours of the morning while the lion, who, having consumed copious amounts of alcohol, was sleeping.

It didn't take long for the apprentice to learn what the kite and unicorn were up to. In-between their love-making, the kite and unicorn let down their guard at the tavern, and within earshot of the apprentice, they discussed the plot to put British rods on the Old South Meeting House in order to attract lightning and burn it down.

A day after the couple's rendezvous in the loft, the unicorn handed the rods to the lion, who then tied them to the kite, and one by one, the kite installed the rods on the Meeting House. The whole process took two days, and then it was complete.

The kite had barely finished installing the last of the British lightning rods with the knobby ends when Revere and his apprentice acted. Revere mounted his old gray mare, the granddaughter of the horse he had ridden during his famous Midnight Ride and galloped through the streets shouting in his hoarse voice: "The British are coming. The British are coming. Stay away from the Old South Meeting House at all costs. They intend to burn it down like they did The White House!"

None of the citizens believed that the British were coming, nor did they understand the principles of electricity that Revere tried to explain to those who stopped to listen to him.

While Revere was crisscrossing the city, the apprentice was busy with the unpleasant task of informing the lion he had been cuckolded.

"You've been had, sir," the apprentice told the lion as the cuckolded husband sipped a beer at the tavern. "Your wife has been unfaithful to you."

"She would never do such a thing," the lion retorted angrily. "You are just jealous that you don't have a wife yourself."

"See for yourself." The apprentice threw down a pile of letters in front of the lion.

The lion poured through the letters, and as he did so his mane stood up. He banged his fist on the table, causing his crown to fall off. Dropping the parchment, the lion sprung from the table and scaled the ladder to the loft. The apprentice heard a brief struggle and a shriek, but before he could act, the deed had been done, and the unicorn was dead. The lion rushed down the ladder, pushed the apprentice aside, and made for the Old South Meeting House with his late wife's horn in his mouth. Once at the Old South Meeting House, the lion clawed his way up the exterior, and one by one he removed the British lightning rods. In their place, he inserted his wife's horn on the steeple. He was determined to both burn down the Old South Meeting House and desecrate her memory.

"You betray your husband in life and so you shall betray your country in death," the lion cried. "Your horn is pointy like an American rod, not round like a British one. Still, you may redeem yourself. Let us see if you can aid in the destruction of the Old South Meeting House." As the lion spoke, the sky turned pitch-black.

The storm poured down with an intensity that the city of Boston had not seen in fifty years.

Meanwhile, the apprentice rushed to the kite's house and informed him of his lover's death, hoping the news would force him to reassess what he had done earlier that day to the Old South Meeting House. The kite threw on his clothes and flew high above it, and when he saw his lover's remains, he howled in distress. Lightning flashed through the sky as the kite soared higher, not wanting his lover's remains to be desecrated despite his hatred for the Puritans.

"Take me instead. Take me instead," the kite wailed, just as a bolt of lightning struck him, and he plummeted to the ground in front of the Old South Meeting House.

As quickly as the storm had arrived it dissipated. The next day the citizens of Boston buried the unicorn and the kite in a common grave in the Old Granary Burying Ground, the same cemetery where Paul Revere would rest in a few years.

The kite was hailed a hero. The lion licked his wound, but neither Revere nor the apprentice was mentioned, and neither was the unicorn's role in the affair. In time, the citizens of Boston built their church of brick, the world grew more knowledgeable about science, and the descendants of the Puritans became the deists the kite had wished they had been.

Swarovski Crystals

Bern, Switzerland, 1916

On February 29, Björk, the youthful brown bear, woke up in the Bärengraben, or Bear Pit, in Bern. As World War I raged in all the countries that bordered Switzerland, the bear ate. He had been gorging himself on nuts, fruits, and even sausages thrown in by onlookers in the early winter months, along with the honey that was procured from a beehive hanging above his enclosure. Björk was not hibernating, not this year. He simply was not in the mood. He was on a mission.

The previous spring, Björk had heard of two incidents that left him determined to be awake on the next leap year. First, the worker bees who lived in the hive told him that when the two new Queens had hatched, they fought to the death and the survivor became their home's new ruler. According to the bees, the fight had been extremely bloody; in fact, there had not been such infighting in their home in a hundred years. The hive had been hoping to surpass Switzerland's record for the most years gone without fighting in a war, but with the renewed bloodshed, this was not possible now. As a result, the hive was in a somber mood.

The second incident involved the celebrities Albert Einstein and Vladimir Ilich Lenin. Björk had recently found an errant piece of paper that had flown out of Lenin's notebook, one that described his plans to return to Russia and start a revolution, whereby he would establish a dictatorship of the working class. Meanwhile, there had been rumors in the local papers that Einstein was on the verge of another scientific breakthrough, The Theory of Relativity, which had piqued the bear's interest.

So why did the Queen bee's fight to the death and the two celebrities' plans cause Björk to wake up from his hibernation in the middle of winter that year? The reason was simple. Björk was determined to see if Swiss society, which outsiders considered so perfect, was as tolerant as it portrayed itself to be. The bear, who resented having to reside in a pit for the visitors' amusement, devised a test to determine the tolerance of his fellow citizens. How would the people react if they saw their town's mascot exercising his liberty to take a simple walk? Would the people of the German Canton of Bern treat him like any other? Would they look upon him as a fellow citizen? Would they chide him and tell him to get back into his pen? He did not know, but he needed to find out.

Björk chose a leap year to try out his plan for one reason: The hands of the Zytglogge Clock Tower, a medieval landmark, had to be changed manually on leap years. The clock, a remarkable contraption that had Julian and Gregorian calendars on it, tended to itself in all other matters, save occasional repairs, oiling, and other maintenance. Björk believed he had an alibi to be out of the Bärengraben, as he was doing a service to his city.

"I'll be back soon," Björk said to a worker bee, and he proceeded to scale the walls of his pit at five in the evening on February 29, 1916. "Let's see how tolerant my fellow countrymen really are."

"I can tell you right now that your exercise is futile," the worker bee commented. "If you want to see how this country behaves, look no further than our hive. Every day we workers and drones serve our Queen without fail. Like Swiss men, we all do our military service and are willing to die for our country by stinging others. We do not welcome outsiders. To the citizens of Bern, you are an invader."

"Ah, yes, but you have experienced civil wars many times," Björk replied.

"I think you are romanticizing your view of your country, but I do not blame you for wanting to get out of the Bärengraben," the worker bee said, and he took his leave to serve his sovereign who had just laid a fresh batch of eggs.

Once outside the Bärengraben, Björk did not have far to walk. His home and the Zytglogge were only half a kilometer from each other, and he had only a few streets to cross. Early twentieth century Bern, while being a hub of technology, still had streets that were predominantly traversed by horses and buggies, and although the roads were in good order, a bear still had to be careful when crossing. Björk knew that he would scare most drivers and could have made his way across the streets unhindered, but he took pains to follow the rules of the road. At the first crosswalk, he made sure that his feet stayed on the black pavement between the white lines so as not to get mud on the stripes that denoted the crosswalk. After having navigated the first street, Björk passed a small park where he happened upon Albert Einstein smoking a pipe and reviewing some of his papers.

"Where are you off to?" the future world-renowned physicist called after Björk, not seeming the least bit alarmed at seeing a fully grown bear walking freely in the capital's streets.

"To the change the Zytglogge," Björk replied. "It is leap year, the hand needs to be changed and no one has done it yet. I do not want our punctual city to be thrown off in any way."

"Doing your civic duty," Einstein chuckled. "In all seriousness that is very nice of you. But I was wondering, could I trouble you to assist me with something?"

"But of course," Björk said, and he stopped in the middle of the second crosswalk. The bear was pleasantly surprised and flattered that one of his fellow citizens requested his aid.

"I am testing one of my new theories," the scientist began. "The Theory of Relativity to be exact. Its basic premise is that the laws of physics are identical across all inertial frames of reference and that the speed of light in a vacuum is the same for all observers regardless of their relative motion or the motion of the source of the light. It just so happens that the hand on the clock would be a perfect object on which to test my theory." The physicist then mounted his bicycle and began to drive around the square gazing at the hand on the clock that Björk was going to change.

Björk finished crossing the crosswalk and started up the stepladder that leaned against the Zytglogge, as the clock was striking six o'clock on that Tuesday. Right on cue, Mars, the deity on the Ptolemaic calendar and the representation of Tuesday, did a dance while the bear continued to climb.

"The clocktower was originally a guard tower, but it was used as a women's prison for maidens who had relationships with priests. Now, it is the central timepiece of the country, a civic landmark," Einstein said as he cycled around the square holding a device that only he, the greatest scientist of all time, could have invented. "Turn the hand slowly," Einstein called to Björk.

Björk did as he was told and then began to climb down the ladder only to hear Einstein call after him. "Incredible. By my calculations from my relative position, the hand is moving one half as fast as yours. Now, I can complete my hypothesis and publish my paper." The scientist took out a camera from his coat and snapped a picture of Björk, who had finished climbing down the ladder and started his journey back to the Bärengraben.

"Where are you going?" Einstein called after the bear.

"Back to the Bärengraben. My experiment is done," Björk called back.

"And I thought I was the biggest experimenter in town," Einstein said, laughing. "Tell me, what is your experiment?"

"I've lived all my life in the Bärengraben," Björk said. "I wanted to see how I would be treated if I acted like a citizen of Bern and not as its mascot. You have answered my question. You have treated me as an equal."

"Did you expect anything else?" Einstein asked.

Björk was just about to answer no when he heard a policeman's brusque voice.

"Halt!" the policeman shouted. "What are you doing out of the Bärengraben?"

Björk was so startled by the officer's tone that his efforts to avoid the lines of the crosswalk failed, and he landed on all fours. "I was just trying to be of service to the city and change the hand of the clock. It is a leap year."

"That is my job, and I would have gotten around to it," the policeman barked. "Now get back to your pen."

Dejected, Björk walked back to the Bärengraben and began to munch on a sausage that had been thrown in by a tourist that morning.

"Well, how did it go?" the worker bee asked.

"Just as you told me it would," Björk replied sullenly as he rested his head on his front paws and lay down like a sphinx. "I was not treated well except by Einstein, the scientist. He treated me decently, but I was able to help him."

"That's more than we bees get." The bee shrugged his wings. "Everyone, even Einstein, considers us pests except for when they raid our hive for honey."

"Well, at least now I have my answer," Björk said. Then he stretched out and tried to go to sleep.

The next morning, hundreds of tourists, more than the normal on a winter's day, came to see Björk at the Bärengraben. Unlike days in the past, the visitors were escorted by the policeman who had chastised Björk the evening before.

"The bear got out of the pen, and I escorted him back," the policeman said proudly.

"But he also helped," Einstein, who had also come to see Björk, countered. "He changed the clock that we hold so dear. I took a photo of him at the Zytglogge, and it was published in today's paper."

"Yes, but that was my job," the policeman said. "We know the purpose of having bears in Bern. Our city's founder proclaimed that the first animal he killed during a hunt would be its mascot. Imagine what the bear would have done had I not been there to escort him back from the Zytglogge. Imagine the injuries he could have caused others had he gone on his walk during the daytime and not in the evening." The crowd nodded in agreement.

For the rest of the day on that cold March 1, a procession of tourists visited the Bärengraben to see the bear who had changed the hand on the Zytglogge. Einstein tossed an apple to him, and Lenin threw a sausage. Björk couldn't sleep with all the pandemonium, and it was not until evening when the crowd finally dispersed that the bear found some peace. Einstein saw the bear was still visibly upset, and he stayed to console Björk.

"I am so sorry this has happened to you," the famous scientist began. "I will stand by you, as you are as much a Swiss citizen as I am." For the next few months, Einstein, instead of going to his study, wrote his papers on a bench next to the Bärengraben. The scientist truly felt sorry for the bear, and when the bear was amenable, Einstein made small talk with him. Tourists came in even greater number, leaving Björk to wonder if it was because of the famous scientist sitting next to him, or if it was because of his exploits with the Zytglogge. Not to mention he wasn't hibernating, and that was a highly unusual circumstance.

Eventually, Björk's jealousy got the better of him. Convinced that his notoriety was due to the scientist, Björk snapped at Einstein and asked him to leave. The scientist obliged. The next day, Einstein boarded a train for Germany, a country he would flee twenty years later, never to return to Switzerland. Björk finally got his sleep and didn't cease his hibernating until late in May. The worker bee was waiting for him.

"I read a newspaper this morning that was blown in from a rubbish bin," the bee began. "There are rumors that Lenin is going to return to Russia to complete his revolution soon."

"My friend," Björk replied, "after what happened a few months ago, the outside world no longer interests me. I will be remembered as the bear who went for a walk on a leap year. At best, my antics will be celebrated only every four years."

"Well, if what the paper says is true, hopefully the Great War will end sooner than later, not that it is directly affecting us. But if the state of affairs at my home is a foreshadowing," the bee gestured to his hive, "we have only one queen this year and no others have hatched, so there is peace."

"I am glad that fortune is smiling on you," Björk replied.

As the months rolled by, the tourists were no longer like the crowds when Einstein visited, but they still came tossing pieces of fruit, nuts, and an occasional sausage to Björk. He would stand and try to catch the food, but his mind was on the Theory of Relativity that Einstein had explained to him.

"I wish that people could see us not as other, but simply different. If only it were just like Einstein's Theory of Relativity, which sees motion and its speed as the same for all, just from different perspectives." Björk made this comment to the bee at the end of one summer in 1939 as the bee flew around the enclosure while a zookeeper raided the hive for honey.

"Still thinking of the scientist that you challenged a couple of decades ago?" the bee asked. "I just read in the paper that he was granted asylum in the United States, after he was exiled from Nazi Germany and declared persona non grata."

"I misjudged him," Björk said. "And I now regret it."

Within months, Europe was once again at war. Two leap years fell during World War II, one in 1940 and the other in 1944. Switzerland remained officially neutral, as it had throughout the war years, even though its financial sector backed the Axis powers. Björk was tempted to be helpful again, but only when the appropriate time presented itself. Perhaps people would then be more sensitive. Still, Björk could not bring himself to leave the Bärengraben to perform, feeling the most innocuous help he could provide was turning the weekday hand on the Zytglogge.

The war ended and Europe rebuilt itself, creating the European Union and establishing one currency for the block, although the Union did not include Switzerland. Nevertheless, Björk saw this development as progress. By now he was a grandfather and his life had improved. Not only was his family growing, but the Bärengraben had been enlarged so that he and his family could go via an underground tunnel to cool off in the river before coming back for the night. The policeman who had escorted him back to the Bärengraben had also retired. Now, his son had taken over his position.

"Perhaps the spirit of the times has changed. Our home has had reforms as well, and the bees have not had a civil war in their hive since the war's end," Björk told his grandson Hans as they listened to the Zytglogge strike twelve in February 1956. "Tomorrow is a leap year. Perhaps you should try what I did years ago and change the week hand on the Zytglogge."

"Do you think the people will accept me?" Hans asked.

"I think there is a good chance, so much has changed in our country. Infighting in the countries around us has stopped, our banks are more transparent, who knows. Why even the crosswalks are different. They are now lined with Swarovski Crystals, ostensibly to make the crossers more visible to automobiles."

"Let's see what happens," Hans said excitedly. "Perhaps I will have better luck than you did."

The next evening, around six o'clock after the sun had already set, on the 29th of February when the tourists had gone home, Hans did what his father had done years before. He climbed out of the Bärengraben and made his way across the two crosswalks.

"Crystals are indeed here," Hans muttered as he attempted to cross the crosswalk without stepping on the lines in much the same way his grandfather had. Hans made it across the first crosswalk with no problem, and then he entered the second crosswalk. Hans was about halfway when the blaring of a horn caused him to run back to the sidewalk. A driver seemingly under the influence had almost hit him. Too traumatized to go on, Hans started running back toward the Bärengraben, but while he was on his way, a policeman caught sight of him.

"What are you doing out of the pen?" the policeman snapped. Before Hans could answer, the policeman grabbed the bear by the collar and dragged him to the edge of the Bärengraben, leaving him to scamper back and relate his woes to his grandfather.

“Back so soon? What happened?” Björk asked as he hugged his grandson.

“A car almost hit me, and had it not been for the crystals, I am sure the driver would not have seen me. And what is more, when the policeman saw the close call, instead of being concerned for my welfare, he brought me back here in much the same way you were long ago.”

Björk shook his head as he consoled his grandson and rocked him to sleep. Soon Björk was asleep too. The next morning the two bears were awakened by the great-great-great-grandson of the bee Björk had spoken with decades before.

“I heard what went on last night, and I am sorry,” the bee began.

“Yes, even though the country is awash with wealth and people have nothing to want for, they still cannot stop acting like animals,” Björk replied.

“I am afraid the same is true with my house. We are animalistic too as we are now embroiled in a war,” the bee replied. “In spite of the fact that we bees are homogenous, one would think this would prevent internal strife. But no, we too are embroiled in war.” The bee flew around Björk and his grandson and continued. “Last night a new queen hatched, and we now have two queens fighting to the death. Until one wins, I am a persona non grata, much like Einstein was.”

“If only his Theory of Relativity were seen by people in their relationship with each other and not just to objects in motion,” Björk mused.

"Ah, life," the bee sighed. "It is all about going through the motions. What is the value?"

Björk, Hans, and the bee were silent, as they watched the sun rise, waiting for tourists to arrive at the Bärengraben to shower the bears with food, as they lounged in captivity in Europe's most peaceful country.

Siberian Samovar

The locomotive stalled ten kilometers outside of Moscow. Their inaugural ride along the Trans-Siberian Railway was supposed to end with great fanfare the next day, and the festivities would be attended by the Tsar himself. Now, in early March, with the ground still frozen, the crew was unsure if they would ever see the great city and the domes of Saint Basil's Cathedral ever again.

The engineer was given the honor of driving the three-car train with only the engine, a coal car, and a small sleeping car in the rear, but now he and his crew were stuck. The engineer, the cook, the priest, and the soldier disembarked from the train, and the cook went to work lighting a fire in the middle of a circle of stumps that he found one hundred yards from where they had stalled. The Trans-Siberian Railway was finished six months before, and many of the trees along either side of the rails had been cut down to create trestles, leaving many fields of empty stumps.

After lighting the fire, the cook went back to the train to prepare the samovar that the crew sipped tea from every night. Blowing on his hands to keep them warm, the cook removed the stack and took some coal from the rucksack and began to fill the chamber with water while putting snow around the stack itself.

"Careful with that. Do not use so much coal. If I can fix the engine, we might be able to go another kilometer or two," the engineer said.

"What is the point? We will still be eight kilometers from Moscow," the cook replied. "It is better to spend our last night out in the wildness, warm and in good company, than to spend it in a freezing train tomorrow."

"He is right," the priest said. He ambled over with the few icons that each crewmate had kept by their cot and began to set them up on each stump around the fire that the cook had built.

"I am not so sure," the engineer said. "Perhaps there will be a miracle. Perhaps the load of coal will carry us the ten kilometers to Moscow rather than the two we have enough for."

"I gave up on miracles," the soldier said as he walked over to the makeshift camp. "After fighting in the Crimean War and praying to *The Black Madonna* before battle, I am the sole survivor of my battalion."

"But you survived," the engineer said.

"Exactly," the solider replied, taking a swig of water from his canteen. "I survived. I'd rather have died with all my comrades or have them living with me. Now, if you will excuse me, I'm going to fetch the tea. It can't take that long for the water to boil." The soldier made his way back to the sleeping car at the rear of the train.

"I find it interesting," the engineer began as he rubbed his hands by the fire, "that all of you, including you, Father," the engineer gestured to the priest, "would choose a more luxurious night tonight over saving your skins tomorrow."

"The samovar is the locomotive of socialization," the cook said. He opened the spout to see if the water was boiling, but it was already hitting the gourd and hissing as it contacted the ice. "Just look at it. It has a smokestack to release steam just like our train over there. Before we started this trip, we made a pact that we would have tea every night and sing songs to stay sane traversing the thousands of lonely kilometers through the unremarkable birch forests."

"Sergei is right," the priest interjected. "God's country may indeed be a beautiful sight to behold, but it is lonely. Thanks be to Him that we had each other for all these months."

"Look, the tea is ready!" Sergei said excitedly as he took the teapot off the stack and turned to the soldier who had just returned from the train. "Mikhail, do you mind fetching the glasses?"

"Not at all. I will also get the bread and sausage we left in the larder," Mikhail said, ever so much a gentleman and not at all annoyed at being asked to return to the train. He dashed off to the caboose and soon returned with four glasses. Pavel, the priest, began the prayers before the icons, and the rest of the crew fell silent as he prayed in the Old Church Slavonic. Then, they began to eat.

"What do you think it would have been like had we made it back to Moscow, Fedya?" Sergei asked the engineer. "Do you think the Tsar would have been there to greet us? After all, he did lay the first piece of wood on the rails in Vladivostok years ago."

"Who knows, who knows," Fedya replied and lit a cigarette, then, taking his binoculars out of a small leather pouch, he looked in the direction of Moscow. "Gentlemen," Fedya said excitedly, "my commanding officer gave me these binoculars during the war, and I can see the dome of Saint Basil's Cathedral and the Kremlin in the distance. We are not that far. Come, let's quit this tea party and try to start the locomotive again!"

"She is running just fine," Sergei replied, and he shoved more coal into the shaft. "This is much smoother than that iron horse over there. Why, in two minutes, we will have more hot water. More tea, anyone?

"Why not," Pavel said. He pulled a small portable balalaika from under his robes and began to sing folk songs, urging the others to join in. Only Fedya didn't participate in the singing and nervously lit another cigarette.

"Aren't you going to offer us some, or are you going to smoke the whole pack yourself?" Mikhail asked the engineer. "Are you going to be that rude?"

"With all due respect." Fedya raised his hands in despair. "It is you all who are being rude. We really do have a chance to make it to Moscow. The locomotive can run on woodchips, which we can gather from the surrounding forest. We might be two or three days late, but we have a fighting chance. Why do you push life away when we may have some left?"

"We are hardly pushing life away," Pavel admonished.

"This is true," Mikhail said, backing up the priest. "We are living what life we have left to the fullest," the solider said, and he poured himself another pot of tea.

"My comrades are right," Sergei broke in. "If anyone is being disrespectful to life, it is you. You seem to enjoy it only when you are in control, but life does not work that way."

"Well, I am not about to give up!" Fedya yelled. "I am going to take the axe in the train closet and chop some branches. Feel free to join me if you choose to stop wasting the coal on that samovar of yours."

"Suit yourself," Sergei called after Fedya. "I am afraid we are not going to be much help. We are going to get out the vodka as well."

Fedya went off into the forest and chopped wood for three hours, returning every so often to the locomotive whose boiler was warm enough to keep him from freezing. As he passed by the makeshift camp, he cursed his comrades who were still drinking and carrying on. Fedya worked through the night until morning. He was carrying his sixth load of wood when he passed the campsite and saw that Sergei, Mikhail, and Pavel had frozen to death, unaware that drinking the vodka could make them impervious to the freezing cold surrounding them.

Cursing, the engineer gathered what little coal was left in the stack and made his way back to the locomotive. For the next six hours, using a mixture of woodchips and the last of the coal, Fedya tried to start the locomotive, but to no avail. Thinking that he would meet the same fate as his comrades, he gathered the icons and began to pray. Then he fired up the samovar and poured himself some tea.

"Perhaps they were right," Fedya muttered as he shivered alone that night. "Am I better off tonight? Yes, I am still alive, but I am lonelier now," the engineer whispered. He set the Samovar in the boiler and lit the coals so that the steam floated up the large smokestack of the locomotive. Fedya then walked outside. It was a clear night, and he could see the millions of stars overhead, a good omen. If a train happened to be coming on the other end, anyone from a nearby village would, by chance, see the steam rising from the smokestack, and perhaps he could be saved. The engineer went to sleep, waiting for what he thought would be his last morning.

When the morning finally arrived, Fedya awoke to the sound of a locomotive coming down the track. Looking through his binoculars, Fedya could not believe it was the Imperial train itself. The Tsar, knowing they were late, had come from Moscow to rescue the crew. The train was perhaps two kilometers away and would be there in five minutes. Fedya looked around for something to present to the emperor, but he found nothing deserving of the Tsar. All the sausage and bread had been eaten, and all the vodka and tea had been drunk.

As the Tsar disembarked from his train, Fedya knelt in the snow and said, "Your majesty, thank God you have come. Were it not for you I would have frozen to death!"

"What happened to your comrades?" the Tsar asked, looking at the frozen corpses. "Have you nothing to greet your Emperor with? No food, no tea, just your genuflections?"

"My crew froze to death," Fedya told the Tsar. "They were convinced that we were not going to make it to Moscow and spent their last night using up all the supplies." He looked away from the Tsar. "They said the samovar was their locomotive even if the actual one was broken."

"And you? What did you do?" The Tsar asked.

"I chopped down some trees in the hope that I could make it to Moscow with the woodchips and the little coal left over from the samovar. But it wasn't to be, so I placed the samovar in the boiler hoping that someone would see the steam."

"And now what do you expect to do?" The Tsar asked.

"Why, to return to Moscow with your majesty, hopefully as a hero."

"Return to Moscow you shall, as a hero you shall not," the Tsar proclaimed. "Perhaps you should have thought of the welfare of your comrades before you left them here to die."

"I had every intention of completing our mission," Fedya protested, "but they were frozen to death by the time I returned from chopping wood."

"Sometimes the rule governing the welfare of the group, illogical as it may seem, is wiser than the individual's rationale," the Tsar said before he turned to one of his orderlies. "Fetch me some tea. And wrap up those bodies in some blankets so they can be given a proper Christian funeral in Moscow." Within five minutes, the tea was prepared, and Fedya toasted his emperor as the two men drank the tea together.

After the engineer's train was turned around, the Tsar did not invite Fedya into the Imperial coach but demanded that he ride in the caboose back to Moscow. The Tsar, his emperor, had made him a laughingstock for all to see and given the samovar a place of honor in his private coach. The Samovar, the little locomotive that Fedya had decried, the one that had been with him the entire journey along the Trans-Siberian Railway, entered the capital in triumph, leaving the engineer to lick his wounds over a cold glass of tea.

The Iguana and the Cigar Workers

Cigar makers are "intellectuals who work with their hands," who toil in "factories that are like colleges with their continuous reading and thinking, and these schools where the hand that folds the tobacco leaf by day, lifts the text by night." –From the Diary of Jose Marti

The scorching sun beat down on the serrated tin roof of the cigar factory behind the bayou in Ybor City. The cigar makers had arrived an hour before the owner unlocked the building, and they saw their beloved Lector Ignacio, a three-foot male iguana with a large dewlap, reading the morning paper on the roof.

Ignacio had used a groove in the structure as an anchor for his fat tail, his dewlap looking like a long, wizard-like beard. He had just finished shedding his skin and was in a lazy mood when Miguel, an ally, spoke to him.

"I am glad it was not cold last night, Señor Lector," Miguel called up.

"I am too, Miguel. I am too," Lector Ignacio responded. "Had there been a cold front, I'd be frozen and would have fallen from the roof. Then you would have had to wait until I was revived by the sun to come here and start reading to you."

"Yes, and the last time that happened it was already noon. The day was half over. Not only that, but you read the same article as you did the other day."

"Perhaps you should vote in another, more consistent Lector," Ignacio chuckled.

"No, we wouldn't dream of it," Miguel, said gesturing to his co-workers who stood around him.

"No, nunca," Miguel's co-workers said in unison.

"No matter what pressure the owner puts us under, you always read to us and tell us what we need to hear," Miguel said. "You are the voice of the working class. You may grow numb from the weather at times, but your heart is always with us."

"Por siempre," the workers again crowed as one.

As the workers spoke, Ignacio began his descent from the roof with the daily paper tucked under his arm, just as the owner of the factory, *Cigarro Excelente*, pulled up in the gravel driveway. He was a light-skinned man dressed in a suit with gold cufflinks, a fedora nearly covering his eyes, and a cigar hung out of his mouth.

"How are we today?" the owner called. He brashly threw the gear into park and stepped out of the car, blowing a plume of smoke where the workers waited. "Ready to meet a new quota?"

The owner proceeded to unlock the factory door and the workers filed in with frowns on their faces.

They felt unappreciated and expendable, Ignacio observed, as he walked behind them.

The day began as it always did, the owner retiring to his office above the factory floor and peering through the glass windows so he could see what was happening below. He noticed Ignacio climb onto a chair and spread the daily newspaper on the cheap pine lectern where he sat every day.

Eager to match their mood with what he was going to read, Ignacio continued to scrutinize the workers. Today was not a day for something light, nor a day for the novels that were among the favorites of cigar workers like *Les Misérables* or *Don Quixote*. The workers needed something that would awaken their feelings of being exploited, giving them the energy to work in the sweltering factory for the next twelve hours.

Ignacio watched as a group of workers spread along their workbenches and picked up the chavetas to cut the tobacco leaves, while their counterparts, the wrapper selectors, spread to the four corners of the factory where mounds of tobacco lay. Newly installed fans whirred from the sides of the factory, and lamps with low-wattage bulbs hung above the benches, setting the stage for the workers' dexterous fingers to create the Corona, Churchill, and Robusto cigars.

As they moved to their stations, Ignacio empathized with them. It was the height of the Great Depression, and they were struggling to make ends meet. They would go home with aching hands while the owner's fingers were developing callouses from counting all the profits that he made off their labor. Most of the workers were illiterate, so the iguana read to them while they worked, and on Sundays he taught classes to help them learn how to read.

Behind the lectern now, Ignacio saw the angst written on the workers' faces, and as the Lector of the factory, his job was to cater to the feelings of the workers, many of whom held left-leaning political views.

"Let's continue stoking the fires of discontent," Ignacio muttered, and turning to the international section of the paper, he began to read. The microphone was perched above the lectern and wired into a series of scratchy, feeble speakers attached by flimsy wire to each corner of the factory. "It was announced by the Roosevelt Administration yesterday that a hundred more tractors will be sold to the Soviet Union paid for in gold bars. The treasury intends to add the gold to the reserves hoping that it will bolster confidence in the dollar."

"I can barely afford the bus to get here," a cigar maker called out as he finished shaping the foot of a cigar.

"Forget the bus, I can't afford rice to feed my children," a wrapper selector quipped from one of the corners of the factory."

"We are paid too little," chimed in a third worker.

"Here, here," the workers shouted in unison as they tapped their chavetas on the workbenches.

Enveloped in clouds of his own cigar smoke, the owner could not observe what was happening on the factory floor, but he heard the shouting beneath him. He threw the newspaper down, almost starting a fire when the ashtray nearly flipped over spilling the contents on the wooden floor.

"What is going on?" the owner fumed as he stood above the workers on his metal platform. "Are you being read those pro-communist newspapers?" The owner clutched the double banister and ran downstairs grabbing the newspaper held like a scroll in Ignacio's tail.

The owner scoured the headline and the text below it, and crumbled it into a ball, threw it on the floor, and stamped on it with his foot. Then the owner turned off the heating lamp hanging above the lectern where Ignacio was stationed.

"Turn the lamp back on," Miguel said. "El Lector will get cold and won't be able to read."

"Turn off the fans you had me install," the owner retorted, "then it will not be too cold for your beloved Lector. I save money or you work diligently without letting these pro-Soviet thoughts enter your inept minds! As if it is the last society or way of life you should wish to emulate! A society governed by the proletariat, pah!" The owner stormed off and climbed the stairs, slamming his office door behind him.

When Ignacio saw the owner at his desk, he reached for *Don Quixote,* one of the many books he kept underneath his lectern. "How about something lighter," he called through his mic. The workers shrugged and went back to rolling their cigars.

Ignacio began to read from where he had left off the previous week. "'Look, your grace,' responded Sancho, 'what you see over there aren't giants—they're windmills; and what seems to be arms are the sails that rotate the millstone when they're turned by the wind." He didn't make it more than a few pages with the heating lamp off, and like a contorted mummy, he fell to the floor.

None of the workers dared to help their Lector for fear of being reprimanded. When the bell rang at the end of the work hours and the owner locked up the factory and drove off in his Bentley, Miguel climbed up a gutter to the roof while his colleagues put apples, mangos, and other fruit in a basket for Ignacio. He saw Ignacio in a dire condition and knew the only way to save him was to place him in the sun. He watched over him, waiting an hour for Ignacio to revive.

"It's funny," Ignacio said as he woke up. "Every time I read something that the owner considers to be objectionable, I feel like Don Quixote, that errant knight who reasons that his failures will amount to a success. While I have not gotten through to the owner that he is exploiting his workers, I try to make the fire in your belly that much stronger. Eventually, my readings will bear fruit."

"They will, El Lector, they will. After today's events, we have decided to strike."

"Strike?" Said Ignacio, startled. "You struck last month when the owner refused to provide me a heating lamp."

"And were the results positive?" Manuel asked.

"Why, yes but—"

"Then what do we have to lose," Miguel said as he slid down the gutter pipe and headed home before Ignacio had a chance to answer.

***

On the day of the strike, Ignacio had intended to skip work to show solidarity, but Mother Nature had other plans. An unexpected cold front had moved in and dropped the temperature into the fifties, making the lizard as frozen as when the heating lamp was turned off.

The owner pulled up in his Bentley, got out, popped the trunk, and pulled out a cigar-wrapping machine inside. "If they are going to strike, I will make sure they are out of a job permanently," the owner muttered as he pulled the machine inside the factory and set it up to see how it worked. For the next three hours, he sat on a stool, feeding tobacco into the machine, cursing as he toyed with the levers only to discover that the machine could make only half the cigars that his workers could make in a day.

"I still need them," the owner said. "But I need them to be productive, not working against me. No more strikes or I'll fire all of them." It was noon and the temperature had risen by twenty degrees. As the owner stepped outside for an afternoon smoke, he tilted his fedora to block out the sun and watched Ignacio stretch as he rubbed his head against the roof.

"Time to shed?" the owner yelled up to him.

"Yes, it's that time again," Ignacio said. "I just hope the workers will be back to feed me as I am getting bigger. Although it is natural for all reptiles to shed their skin, if I do it too much and become too fat, they will think I am joining the middle class."

"Suppose they did not have to? Suppose we all could be winners. Would that change your tune?" the owner asked.

"That would happen only if I owned a factory like you and was rich. Now, reading to the workers I earn my keep, and besides, the workers need me."

"Indeed, they do, just as much as I need them. I'll tell you what," the owner said as he adjusted his fedora to block the glaring sun. "I just installed some machinery, but it will not produce enough cigars to make it worthwhile to fire the workers. I'll let you read what you want if they meet the quotas. Sound like a deal?"

"It does," Ignacio said, and he shimmied down the gutter pipe and made his way across the bayou to tell Miguel the good news.

***

The next day the workers were back. They worked swiftly, relishing in the knowledge that they had won their fight. They could hear each other working across the factory and tapping their chavetas only between readings when Ignacio would climb down from the lectern and rub his body against the lever of one of the machines to work the skin off his body.

"Moving up in the world," Miguel said to Ignacio.

"And the owner is moving down," Ignacio said.

By the time the workday was over, Ignacio had read the international sections of two newspapers to the workers. When the bell rang, they wanted to pay him, but Ignacio politely refused, explaining to Miguel and the workers the new terms of his contract.

"I spoke with the owner yesterday, and we reached an understanding. As long as you meet your quotas, I have been given free-range to read to you whatever you wish. Don't worry, I am still in your corner," Ignacio said as he shed the last of his skin and walked out of the factory leaving a white pile of dead cells behind him. The workers cheered and hung the shed skin behind the lectern in gratitude.

"To a symbol of our labor," Miguel beamed as they left for the night.

The arrangement for the three parties went well. The workers listened to Ignacio and heard what they craved, exciting their nascent egos. While they did not get a raise immediately, they met higher quotas and took home more money. With more cigars to sell, the owner doubled his profits, and Ignacio feasted on mangoes and the choicest fruits the workers gave to him.

As Ignacio ate more, he gained weight and had to shed his skin more often. The entire process was arduous, sometimes taking him out of commission so he couldn't read to the workers. He could hardly lift his head and speak into the microphone. In addition, he ate more extravagantly, he gained weight to the point that he became lethargic, and when he did read, he no longer had the vibrant voice full of conviction the workers were used to.

"El Lector está gordo," one of Miguel's colleges quipped to him as they left the shop for the night. "Y no puede trabajar."

"Somos flacos," Miguel responded. "Y trabajamos mucho."

***

Summer passed into fall, and the temperatures remained warm enough, so Ignacio did not need a heating lamp. The workers had Labor Day off and the factory was closed, but the owner used the holiday to surreptitiously install a second cigar-wrapping machine. For as long as he could remember, the owner had wanted to convert his factory to full automation. Not only could he mass-produce more cigars, but also his profits would triple with the costs he would save by dismissing his labor force. Without Ignacio to galvanize them with his oratorial skills, they would become fatalistic and accept their lot—or so the owner believed. They would slink quietly away from Ybor City in search of work at less developed factories where their wages were lower and no lector to read to them.

Ignacio, exhausted and demoralized, listened from the roof as the owner shouted with glee, "Tomorrow I can fire all the workers and two machines will manufacture all the cigars!" Saying nothing to Ignacio, the owner closed the factory and drove home.

After the holiday, Miguel and the workers showed up eager to work. The air was unusually cold, and Ignacio was temporarily incapacitated. "We have hit our quotas for two straight months," Miguel said. "Perhaps we should ask for a raise. We have worked so hard."

"If you keep raking in more money, soon you will join the middle class," Ignacio said.

"I know, I know," Miguel beamed. "Who knows. Soon we may have to change what you are reading to suit our new status."

For two hours the workers waited in gloomy fog for the lights of the Bentley to pierce the haze, but no automobile came. When at noon the owner finally showed up, the workers sensed something was wrong.

"Why are you late?" Miguel asked brazenly.

"I only need four hours to make my quota," the owner said and walked through the crowd of workers and unlocked the factory.

"Did you hire other workers? Will our wages go down?" Miguel asked.

"No, in fact I don't need any of you workers. Yesterday, I purchased a second machine, and all of you are fired." The owner walked inside the factory, removed the shedding skin, and tossed it at Miguel's feet before slamming the door in his face and locking the building from the inside.

"Machines," Miguel muttered to the others. "Machines and now there are two. I am sure Ignacio never envisioned this as we were all becoming winners. We made more money, and Ignacio read to us during our long working hours. How life has a way of being so cruel." It began to rain, an ominous sign for the iguana, who would freeze in the cold drops falling on him.

Miguel and the workers looked at the mucky ground, downcast and broken, and Miguel thought that even Ignacio's readings couldn't stop the owner from double-dealing. Just then, the iguana fell off the slippery roof and landed unceremoniously in the center of where the workers stood.

"Should we revive him?" a worker asked. "I am sure the owner will let us take the lamp—"

"Yes, we should.," Miguel said. He picked up Ignacio and held him under his shirt against his warm skin. "All along he wanted to help us and was doing so, but he could not foresee the owner's buying a second machine. Just as we were paid more, he was shedding his skin, reading the daily tracts to us, and eating an iguana diet, losing weight. Now, both of us have been left out in the cold, Ignacio literally. He stiffens up, and he cannot function. Remember when the owner snatched the lamp away from him and he could not read to us?"

After he finished speaking, Miguel led the workers away with Ignacio under his shirt, who soon revived.

"Where are we going?" Ignacio asked.

"To find somewhere else to work, and if we are paid half, so be it, but you will still be our Lector," Miguel said.

"Cigar markers are intellectuals who work with their hands, who toil in factories that are like colleges with their continuous reading and thinking," Ignacio said. "These are schools where the hand that folds the tobacco leaf by day lifts the text by night."

The Endgame

Observer in the Audience

I would have anticipated many things, but not the scenario in front of me, at this Grandmaster Championship Game Six in 2021. First, I would never have imagined the eighteen-year-old with the pince-nez to have come this far against the Grandmaster. He has won six games in a row, and were he to win this game, he would be the youngest upstart to dethrone a sitting champion. Second, I had never thought that this game was going to end the way it was wrapping up. The rogue had come out swinging too hard for his own good, and now because of perhaps an overzealous impatient mind, that firepower was too much to bear, and he, the player of the white pieces, had set up a stalemate scenario for the Grandmaster who controlled the black ones. Third, in all my years having garnered a coveted seat at these championships, whether they were held in Reykjavik, Vienna, or here in Berlin, I had never been among a crowd that looked so disappointed.

In this match, the sixth one, the one in which the young upstart has the chance to shut the Grandmaster out, the twenty-five or so spectators crane their necks from their leather chairs, watching every move that the players make. I watch as the players digest them, as they wince, as they gesticulate internally all the feelings they cannot emote out of respect to the venue. I have sweated for the past six hours and forgone frequent calls of nature, and even when a ten-minute intermission was called when the air conditioning broke, I did not take the opportunity to walk around Alexanderplatz, the famous square named after Tsar Alexander I of Russia, to commemorate a visit to the city, to inhale some fresh air coming from a southern wind off the river Spree. I am so captivated by the scenario in front of me that I cannot bear to leave my chair. Unlike my companions whose disappointment is palpable, as I have said, I find the prideful behavior of the youth a case worthy of a textbook that I might present to my students at university when I go back to teach in a few days.

I glance at the clock. There are only three minutes until the youth must either extend his hand and offer a draw, or, if his cockiness really has gotten to his head, he could allow the time to elapse, tempt fate, and go into tomorrow's match. I have been sitting for almost six hours. The young upstart could easily have put me and my fellow observers out of our misery three moves ago, but he is in no mood to do so. Had this been a football match, at least half the fans would have left by now, but the conventions of The Game of Kings do not permit this, so I wait and watch Narcissus. My once zestful zeal for his success is evaporating rapidly. He has six more minutes to make his move or resign, and I have started to wonder if he will choose the latter.

Click White's Turn to Move

You spend countless hours analyzing sixty-four squares. Your eyes traverse the ranks and files as you hope to climb the former. You start to rise amongst your friends in the school cafeteria, then you move into public parks, then to formal clubs as you begin to establish a name. As your name begins to grow, you must give up other pleasures you once had. Socializing goes out the door, the friends you once shot pool with at the bar are yesterday's news.

You pay lip service to your girlfriend's feelings, sleeping with her maybe once a week, telling her you love her as you are consumed by holding court with the same sixteen set of pieces every night. You tie them and your mind up in knots as you move them around the board in different combinations, knowing that fortunes are to be made and lost on your ability to manipulate them and exploit them during a game. With a microcosm of feudal society at your command, you try to dismember your opponents. You try to uphold the ancient régime's social contract on your end while annihilating another's.

Such actions, such social revolutions don't happen in the real "civilized world," or at least that is what you are taught in the public school, which goes to great efforts to show how advanced Western Society is. That's why it's exciting for people to watch you play. They aren't about to pack their bags and go off to some god-forsaken place torn by war and strife, and you certainly aren't either. You defeated a grandmaster in the first six games while playing on the black side, which statistically has a greater chance of losing, and doing so in this political climate only upped the stakes, and now you are expected to extend your hand, to capitulate. To come to terms with the fact that you will have to sit down across from this balding, bulbous individual for another six to eight hours yet again.

Your hands sweat. They grow clammy. The whole situation is being filmed, and to preserve a modicum of dignity, you'd rather relieve them of their excess sweat on the defunct society you have been commanding for the past quarter of a day rather than extend your hand prematurely in offering a draw, no matter how much you respect and revile simultaneously. Your hand briefly fondles the new queen that you procure by trading in a pawn. The transfiguration, while seeming like a good move at the time, now spells your doom for the day, but you're not ready to concede. You punch the clock, not with the confidence you had a move or two before, but like some clerk clocking in for a day of work, it is just a means to end.

All the grandiosity that you had dreamed of just minutes before has flown out the window. You keep getting in your own way. You resolve to move the lone knight, the one that has occupied the black squares during the game, the errant Don Quixote. You move him behind the old queen, the one you started the game with, so she is surrounded by her confessor, her bishop, a pawn, her page, and the knight. Only her husband the king languishes back on the left side of the board, gazing down a file directly at the new queen you just acquired by trading in one of your remaining pawns.

Click Black's Turn to Move

[In White's Camp]

"How could this have happened?" a white knight asks a bishop. Of the original middle ranking pieces, they were the only two that remained after some six hours of play. "I spent the last three hours by your side looking at your Book of Hours, saying my Hail Mary's, and what do I have to show for it?"

"Perhaps had his majesty not taken a mistress—" the bishop gestures with his crozier to a second queen who occupied square b8—"divine providence would not be weighing against us."

"I knew I should not have allowed his majesty to castle on his own side of the board," the queen mutters as she brushes her locks from her eyes. "Had we all closed ranks, perhaps he would have focused on the bigger prize, dragging his archnemesis home in victory."

"At least your recompense will be that tomorrow you can start again a monogamous couple and face the minions together," the knight says.

"He will just do it again, once unfaithful, always unfaithful," the original Queen scoffs as she cocks her head back in the direction of her husband.

"It is still beyond me as to why our master does not call the game," a pawn comments. "It would put all of us out of our misery."

Still Black's Turn to Move

[In Black's Camp]

"It appears that we will live to see another day," the castle says to the king, who has been leaning on his scepter during the game, but only now does he do so with a dejected grin. It's the type of grin that one might see on someone who had hit rock bottom as they do their best to laugh off their woes.

"Yes, but at what cost?" the king asks. "Aside from a roof over my head, in the guise of you, I have lost everything. All my sons have died in battle. My spiritual counselors, they too, have met their maker, not to mention my wife is gone. We may be coming out of this game intact, but this is not the case for my psyche. The previous skirmishes were swift. Yes, I lost my dignity in front of my court and in front of my wife, but I never had to be the last one standing."

"Under my ramparts you fall and under them you will rise again tomorrow," the castle replies. "That is unless our opponent chooses to forfeit the game."

As the castle says these words, the king moves behind him, taking shelter under his eaves on whose corners were gargoyle-shaped figures. Only a day ago the king had employed these grotesques to gaze menacingly at his opposite number when checkmate was called. Now the gargoyles sing hymns; they attempt to soothe their king as he mourns his court and dreams of better days, both past and hopefully to come.

Click White's Turn to Move

[In White's Camp]

"One cannot help but admire our opponent's leader," the bishop comments. "He has lost everything save his home, and he still goes behind it, negating all the attention. While he may be the most important piece on the board, he still tries to give the impression that the full court, something bigger than himself, is at stake."

"You give him far too much credit," the queen snaps. "He would be just as much of a philanderer as my husband had he been in skilled hands."

"Perhaps, my lady," a knight comments, "but the dysfunction that plagues our house seems to have eluded his."

Still White's Turn to Move

You have waited for your opponent to read the writing on the wall for the past hour, yet for whatever reason he apes being illiterate. You and he both know his only option is to offer a draw, unless he wants to forfeit, and that you will meet again on the proverbial field of battle tomorrow. You've been through the mud, thoroughly humiliated by the young upstart who already has sullied your record and reputation. You are worn down, psychologically broken. Your chance to fight again another day is through no skill of your own, but rather your opponent's overconfidence and carelessness. He may look like an ass today, but you look like the bigger one; you have the foolhardier track record for the week. You wait for the sweaty hand to be extended, and as you do, you take your handkerchief from your breast pocket and begin to polish your glasses. They are not foggy, but the alibi to relieve your hand from its own sweat has been established. You lie in wait for a reprieve you probably never should have gotten.

Final Minute for White to Move

You are swallowing hard. How could this have happened? You have sacrificed your best years for this moment. If you win tonight, you would consider hanging up a shingle and having a normal life. You'd try to salvage your relationship with your girlfriend; you would retrain yourself in the art of socializing with friends. Maybe you would start with a beer under the Brandenburg Gate to loosen up, as you feel you have forgotten how to relate to others. You now must save face each second that ticks by, making you look more and more foolish in front of people you should not care about, but you do, even if their interest in you is just as superficial as yours has lately been in the friends and family. As you debate what to do with your right hand, the one you use to move the pieces, you hold it in cage, in your pocket. You know it must come out of its suffocating sauna-like prison, sweaty, either to make a move or to be offered to your opponent in a draw; you are conscious of how it will feel to your opponent when you shake, but you couldn't care less. You scowl as you prepare to take it out and offer it to your adversary in a draw.

Final Thirty Seconds for White to Move

I see that Narcissus is starting to crack. I see him look at the clock, then at his queen, then back at the clock again. He cranes his neck, going back and forth across the ranks and files of squares, analyzing every move once again, although it will not give him another result than the rank-and-file stalemate. The finale that every spectator hates. The anticlimactic ending makes me wonder if purchasing tickets to today's game was worth it. I watch as the White player surveys the board again, this time more slowly. He realizes there is no way out. The hand is coming now, slowly, out of the pocket. He extends it toward the Grandmaster like the prodigal son returning from having been out in the world. The Grandmaster, who has been polishing his glasses, looks somewhat surprised. He will not have to wave a white flag today.

I watch as he puts the cloth back in his breast pocket and then as he extends his own hand like a shark eager to eat its prey. I watch the hands clasp. Was the shake hard? Who knows. Both men appear stoic in their expressions, but both are mentally broken. They will take up arms again tomorrow. I get up from my seat, dust myself off, and go for the walk I should have taken hours ago along Alexanderplatz, a square named after a king who, unlike his counterpart on the board, burned his own castle Moscow to the ground, when an overconfident Napoleon invaded his homeland two hundred years ago.

Lviv's Lions

Or When the Moscow Circus Came to Town, We Expected it to Behave

Unlike its easterly counterpart, Lviv had not been scarred by the war. The city, set on the Poltva, an underground river, had more sculptures and images of a lion per capita than any other metropolis, and it was not about to fall.

"When the Moscow Circus comes to town, we expect it to behave," a weathervane in the image of a lion commented from the window of the history museum to his counterpart on the side of Boim Chapel in Cathedral Square.

"I am not sure you or I are in a position to best make that assumption," said Lev the Lion perched on the exterior of the chapel. "We know the reason why you are attached to the wall of the museum. You would always fall off the roof of city hall when bad fortune loomed, and my chapel was never consecrated by the bishop who saw the fresco of the devil smiling from under a chair that Judas is sitting on. Having already received the thirty pieces of silver for his betrayal, Judas was hardly in a benevolent mood."

"Well, I will not let them be ringmasters to us. Now, keep your vigil and your weapon clean and watch over the city. It is only a matter of time before the Russians move on us like they have in Mariupol and Kyiv," the weathervane said.

"Indeed, indeed," Lev said as he blinked his eyes, and an uncomfortable amount of snow fell from his eyelashes. The lions of Lviv, which adorned the emblem of the city, banks, park benches, and wells, stood guard and cradled their machine guns as refugees from the east of the country took shelter in gymnasiums and other spaces that had been converted to house them. A strict curfew was enforced, and the streets were deserted until six o'clock the next morning.

The hours droned slowly, and the lions struggled to keep their eyes open, some even drifting off to sleep, although they were supposed to be on sentry duty. It was only when Lev caught something bright red out of the corner of his eye that he was roused from his sleep.

"Halt, who goes there? Why are you out during curfew?" the lion said, squinting his eyes, trying to see the two, red-nosed figures make their way toward him from across Rynok Square. Both figures were dressed like clowns and looked dubious at best. The fatter and shorter of the two sported a red nose and a red wig, and makeup covered his face and neck. He was dressed like your typical *r'izhii*[1], a lower-class Auguste clown, with his tattered clothes, ripped-up checkered vest, and oversized loafers that made him trip as he slid in the

---

1 Russian folk clown

snow. Accompanying him and holding him up was the second of the pair, a lanky white-faced clown who wore an elegant red wig, his face and neck also painted with makeup.

"Forgive our trespassing," the overweight clown began. "I am Sergei, and this is Vladimir. We are refugees from the Donbas [2] region and we are looking for lodgings in the Hotel George."

Humored by the two buffoons who brought a microcosm of cheer to the city's atmosphere, the lion lowered his firearm and smiled. "It is two more blocks down the street then hang a right, but I doubt there are any vacant rooms. This city has been converted into a displaced persons camp, but you are welcome to check."

"Spasiba[3]," Sergei said, the last syllable of the word barely audible as he was elbowed in the ribs by his companion.

"No, Dyakuyu[4]," Vladimir said.

"You are welcome. If you are stopped by anyone else, tell them Lev sent you and tell the receptionist I say hello."

"Will do," Vladimir replied.

Lev watched the two clowns continue down the street as he cradled his machine gun, trying to stay awake.

The two clowns used Lev's name to ask for a room and were immediately shown to one that was used by the staff of the hotel.

"I didn't give any of the refugees this room because it is only for our use. But since so many of us are at the

2 Region of eastern Ukraine where many native Russian speakers live.
3 Thank you in Russian
4 Thank you in Ukrainian

front and you are an acquaintance of Lev, you can have it for the night," the receptionist said.

"Thank you," Vladimir replied. He took the bed by the window leaving the one by the door for Sergei. Because of the fear of air raids, Vladimir lit a match and held it up to the wall until he saw two buttons with the words *kurtyna*[5] written below them.

"Let's put it to the test," Sergei said. "I know the women have gone off to fight in the east, but surely there are some still here." The short clown reached his chubby fingers toward the projectiles on the wall.

"No, no," Vladimir said as he slapped his colleague's hand away. "Not until our job is done. We are in the circus, remember, and we have a mandate from Moscow to co-opt the people, to coerce them to surrender. We can reward ourselves later once the job is done. We were not received well in Kyiv, Kharkiv, or Mariupol for that matter, and I believe it's because we lack the lions in our show. We will co-opt them to join, which is why we have come to Lviv."

"Fine, who are we bringing in first?" Sergei asked.

"The tigers," Vladimir replied. He dialed a number on the phone while Sergei looked out the window on the main square where the statue of Taras Shevchenko, Ukraine's national poet, still stood proudly as his country crumbled around him.

"I just spoke with the crew," Vladimir said as he hung up. "The train made it to the station. We will first bring in the tigers, then the monkeys, then the elephants, and

5 Curtain in Polish as Lviv was part of Poland until after WWII. The word "kurtyzana" means courtesan in the same language. When he stayed in the hotel, the writer Count Aleksey Konstantinovich Tolstoy misread the word "kurtyna" as the "kurtyzana" and wrote that visitors to the hotel merely had to push a button by which they could obtain female company.

then the bears if the lions don't rejoin the circus after those acts. Then, we will do our act and once the job is done, we can reward ourselves. Now, get some sleep. We have a long day tomorrow." Vladimir blew out the match and fell asleep. Sergei soon followed leaving the lions to keep watch over the city.

In the morning, Vladimir and Sergei began to set up shop around Rynok Square, which was filled with empty baby carriages, a hundred and nine of them, symbolizing the number of infants that had been killed so far. As the clowns began to move the carriages, the people started to protest.

"Don't you know what these strollers represent?" an elderly woman asked indignantly. "There is one for each child who has been killed in the war with the Russians."

"Don't worry about the dead," Vladimir chided. "Besides, children love the circus, and we have brought a live one to Lviv."

"Yes, don't worry. We will put them back after the show is over," Sergei added.

The adults of the city were not about to relent, but when a newsboy announced that the train was in the station laden with wild animals, the children clamored to see them, and the city's residents parked the strollers by Boim's Chapel. As if on cue, half the lions that adorned the exterior of the chapel handed their firearms to a group of university students who continued to rock the strollers back and forth as seriously as they had during their evening vigil of mourning for the lost infant souls.

The city, whose population had ballooned over the past month since the outbreak of the war, struggled to accommodate all the spectators, which included not only Lviv's inhabitants but also refugees from the eastern part of the country. The spectators made the best use of the city's limited space so all could get a good view of what was about to happen in Rynok Square. They turned to the Old Jewish quarter that housed the once-ostracized Jewish population. Confined to a compact section of the city where space was in short supply, they made creative use of the buildings that had ceilings and floors of different heights. No longer inhabited, the Old Jewish Quarter had become a tourist attraction, but with the circus in town, it was temporarily reverted to its old use.

The city officials made up the front row of seats, slabs of pine that had recently been cut down to make coffins for what were expected to be many deaths and laid across makeshift iron tank-traps to block invading Russian armored vehicles. These rudimentary benches were set up along the perimeter of Rynok Square where statues of Greek Gods stood haughtily with their backs to city hall.

"They don't approve of us watching this entertainment during such grave times," the mayor quipped to the city comptroller.

"They never approved of anything because they always had their backs to the hall," the comptroller replied before being cut off by the voice of Vladimir booming through a bullhorn.

"Ladies and Gentlemen of Lviv, I, Vladimir, and my assistant, Sergei, would like to welcome you to the

Moscow Circus. You are our fourth stop as we make our way through Ukraine. We have been to Kyiv, Kharkiv, and Mariupol, where I must admit, we were not well received, but we hope our fortune will change. Our show is a series of four acts, after which we expect our missing compatriots, the lions, will join us as we move on to Cracow."

"Why were you not well received? Did you not behave?" the weathervane lion called out from the ledge on the museum, whose door had been thrown open so older spectators could gather in the foyer to avoid the snow.

"Sergei, Sergei," Vladimir hissed as he beckoned to his assistant, "is that not the lion who used be on top of the city hall? The one that was removed because he falls whenever something bad is about to happen to the city?"

"Yes, according to the guidebook I read on the train, I believe it is," Sergei replied.

"Then come, let's install him back to his rightful place," Vladimir said as he hit his counterpart on his backside, causing him to fall in the snow. Chuckles erupted from the crowd and Sergei turned as red as his nose. He dusted himself off, unbuttoned his vest, and pulled a long handkerchief from his breast pocket with the light blue and golden-yellow colors of Ukraine. The audience burst into applause.

While Sergei was entertaining the crowd, Vladimir used the opportunity to steal into the museum and unscrew the weathervane from the wall, but as he did so, the cub scratched the ringmaster. "I expected you to behave," the juvenile lion growled.

"Relax, your compatriots seem to be enjoying the show, now cooperate," Vladimir said and loosened the final screw that held the lion on the wall. Returning to the Rynok Square, he handed the weathervane to Sergei, who had commandeered a volunteer who had suspended the long handkerchief on the roof of city hall.

"Go get the tigers ready," Vladimir said, and he began to climb city hall while hanging on to the weathervane. The crowd below craned their necks and yelled catcalls at him, but eventually they clapped, when, after several near falls which would have cost him his life, Vladimir succeeded in placing the weathervane on top of city hall.

"Ladies and gentlemen, I announce our first act, the tigers, our guided missiles." Swinging a rope-hoop covered with wax and doused in kerosene, Sergei prominently lit it ablaze and summoned the first tiger to climb on top of a wooden crate labeled "ammunition product of the USA," which he had dragged from the edge of Rynok Square.

Sergei noticed that the audience was fearful of the blazing rope-hoop and decided he needed to calm them down. "Don't worry," he said. "Our tigers are highly trained and will not cause any collateral damage."

"What damage will they cause in the first act?" the mayor called from the stands.

"Oh, nothing. Don't worry," Sergei said, but then he made the mistake of removing his belt and brandishing it like a whip, causing his pants to fall and revealing several stitched-hearts undergarments. Surrounded by the laughter in the audience, Sergei made another dire mistake: He caused the whip to go limp instead of cracking it so that the tigers would jump through the hoop, when instead, one tiger, chasing after the end of the belt, grazed the edge of the hoop and set his tail ablaze.

"Don't worry," Vladimir called as some young men rushed after the tiger. "The snow will douse the flames."

The wounded tiger held his tail aloft as he fled the circus and made it as far as the interior of the Stefanyk Library, one of the most renowned libraries of scientific works in the country. There, the tiger set several priceless manuscripts on fire before the caretaker threw his morning coffee on the beast to stop the blaze.

Upon being relieved of its burning tail, the tiger dashed across Rynok Square and headed toward the statue named after Adam Mickiewicz, Poland's national poet, with conscript soldiers chasing after it.

"There goes our culture," the mayor said.

"Science is science. It is universal," the comptroller said.

"That's what Putin would say about Russians and Ukrainians. We are one people. Do you really want to buy into that?" the mayor replied.

"Perhaps we won't be the only victims of culture annihilation," the comptroller said. He took out his binoculars and looked toward Mickiewicz Square only to spot the tiger halfway to the pedestal and the soldiers ready to pounce.

"We apologize for the technical difficulties," Vladimir said through his bullhorn, "but I assure you there will be no more mishaps. Our next act is the monkey bombs." The impromptu ringmaster pulled a black sheet from atop a large cage to reveal several gibbons and other new world primates with prehensile tails. Each primate held a book by a famous Russian author: a white gibbon with Ivan Turgenev's *Fathers and Sons,* a famous treatise on nihilism, and a howler monkey with Leo Tolstoy's *Anna Karenina*.

"What are they going to do? Read those tracts of misery about how every happy family is alike and get us to agree to be part of Russia?" the comptroller asked.

"I don't know, I just hope they don't let them out of the cage like the tiger was," the mayor replied. "After that snafu, I don't trust the two clowns running this circus."

The mayor's alarm was right on target. The bewildered adult crowd watched as Vladimir undid the latch, while the children who were enjoying the show laughed and waited for the ringmasters to amuse them some more. As soon as the latch was release, as if on cue, the monkeys ran down Shevchenko Boulevard toward the monument of Taras Shevchenko, Ukraine's national poet. Once there, the monkeys scaled the statue set on an obelisk-like platform and spread out along Taras' arms, the white gibbon perched atop the crown of his head. In the midmorning sun, the monkeys opened their books and leafed through the pages.

"First they destroy our discoveries, which you say are universal, but now they attack our language," the mayor quipped.

"You are right," the comptroller sighed. "I do not see a single book by one of our authors, but then again, would you really want a monkey to be the standard-bearer of our literature?"

"No, I don't think you are right. Look," the mayor said as he took out his own set of binoculars that had been issued to him by the army. "The children down the street are throwing bananas at the apes, and they are dispersing." The mayor cupped his hands around his mouth and shouted to Vladimir and Sergei, "Hey, buffoons, I thought you said there would be no more foul-ups."

"Ah, you know monkeys. They are so closely related to humans that they have a mind of our own. They are autonomous," Vladimir boomed in the bullhorn, interrupting the conversation between the mayor and the comptroller. "Have no fear, for the next act we bring you the tanks, the elephants, which you know are highly intelligent but lack the reasoning of monkeys."

"This could be a bad thing," the comptroller huffed.

"Indeed," said the mayor. "Just look what happened in Mariupol. The Russians shelled the city from ships in the Sea of Azov. The sailors were so detached that they could not even see their targets, out of sight, out of mind, with no human connection—" The mayor's philosophizing was cut short when he saw elephants walking down the street from the direction of the train station. Dressed in an ornate glittery saddle, one elephant pushed a massive ball in front of itself, while the rest of the pachyderms released their bowels in the street. The elephant bringing up the rear that Sergei was riding went as far as to enter the Latin Cathedral and relieve itself next to the foot of the altar. The sacrilegious incident was relayed to the mayor and comptroller when the caretaker of the chapel took it upon himself to cycle the short distance to inform the authorities of his disgust at the debasement of his house of God.

"Perhaps they really do want to restore communism," the mayor quipped.

"Have they not read their own literary giant, Fyodor Dostoevsky, who famously said that without religious values everything is permissible?" the comptroller asked.

"Perhaps they read it too closely and are taking it literally," the mayor replied.

The rest of the elephant troop, which was commandeered by young conscript Russians from Siberia and looked like they were in a drunken stupor and unsure of what they were supposed to be doing, performed their act. With the lead elephant balancing his front legs on a massive ball, and the other elephants balancing on their backs or on other elephants, the Russian soldiers managed to get them into formation around the perimeter of the Rynok Square before they began their trumpeting. The children laughed, unaware of what the elephant had done in the cathedral, and soon were ushered out of the Square and headed to the train station.

"You see," Vladimir said to the remaining audience, beaming, "no collateral damage there. Even the children had laughed." The ringmaster adjusted his red nose, which was starting to fall from his face due to the weather increasing ten degrees over the past hour. "Bring in the bears," he said. "They are just coming from the local cemetery!" As soon as he said these words, a trio of bears came riding their tricycles from the direction of Lychakivske Cemetery. They carried large Russian flags in one hand and steered their tricycles with the other.

As they entered Rynok Square waving their Russian flags, the bears rode in circles around each statue of the Greek gods. Upon hearing that they had come from the cemetery, the local priests from the Orthodox and Catholic denominations crossed themselves while tears ran down their faces due to the profanity they had witnessed.

"Don't worry," Sergei shouted as he emerged from the crowd and grabbed the bullhorn from Vladimir. "I made sure they danced on the graves to the song "Kalinka"[6]

"First, they take away our culture, then our language, and now they desecrate our dead. How much worse can it get? I want to spit in the ringmaster's face," the mayor fumed.

The bears lasted the longest of all the acts, but finally, a clever priest enticed them with honey fetched from the city's open-air museum, a fifteen-minute tram ride from the city center. Smelling the sweetness, the bears took off in the direction of the priest who began to walk back to the park on foot.

Not rattled by the bears running after the priest and the nectar, Sergei and Vladimir proceeded to their final circus performance: the lions. "Ladies and Gentlemen," Sergei boomed through the bullhorn, "our Moscow Circus wouldn't be complete without this one final act performed by the lions."

---

6 A famous Russian nationalistic song about a snowball tree commonly played when good fortune happens.

"Yes, which is why we are here," Vladimir gestured to the lions. "Although world-renowned, our circus isn't complete without you. Surely, you can now see that we all are on the same team and have the same goals in life. Would you care to join us?"

"We expected you to behave," a voice from the lion on the weathervane cried from atop city hall.

"Yes," the lion on Boim's Chapel chimed in.

"Instead, you desecrated our city and the memories of our loved ones," the faces of lions said in unison, located on the arms of benches which ran around the perimeter of the Rynok Square.

"You are a disgrace," a lion on a bicycle on the roof of the city's main bank chimed in. "I say we throw them out of town. What do you all think? Let's take a poll!"

Vladimir and Sergei did not hang around to find out the result of the poll. As the mayor counted hands, the two snuck through the crowd and returned to Hotel George, vacant now that everyone had been outside watching the circus. The two clowns made their way to their room only to be surprised the six men who had been riding the circus elephants at Rynok Square were also there.

"Push the button, push the button!" Vladimir yelled. "Don't let them see us. Thank God they have democratic values and decided to take a poll. Were they authoritarians like us, we'd have been dead by now!"

"We were waiting for you, ringmaster," said one of the six men. "Believe me, we wanted to push the button for a long time. It is time we are rewarded with something for our services," the Siberian who had been riding the lead elephant in the pachyderm troop said.

"I hope the woman is blond," one soldier broke in.

"I prefer brunettes," said another.

"Idiots," Vladimir scoffed as he slammed the button. Kurtyna is curtain in Polish, but you country bumpkins from Siberia would not know that!"

"Do you think the people at Rynok Square know we are here?" Sergei asked anxiously. "Should they find us, I would not put it past them to lynch us from a lamppost."

"No," Vladimir replied as he peeked out the window and saw the whole city running down the street in the direction of the train station. "They are running toward the train station."

"So, maybe the lions will join the circus. Then, our prestige can be restored," Sergei said beaming. "If we can just—"

Sergei's voice trailed off when a loud clang came from the direction of the center of Rynok Square causing Vladimir to look out the window again only to spy that the weathervane, the one he had erected on top of the building, had fallen to the ground.

"That only happens when something bad is about to befall the city," Vladimir said. "Come, let's go to the train station."

"But we are risking—"

"No, we are not—" Vladimir cut off the soldier and took out his phone and made a call.

The train station was chaos. All the animals had been let loose and the lions shepherded women and children like lambs into the circus car as they brandished their firearms to keep men back.

"Men cannot leave. They must fight! Only woman and children can go to Cracow!" the lion from Boim's Chapel said and fired warning shots into the air.

"And I thought the Lviv lions were tame," Sergei said as he and Vladimir along with the six soldiers snuck into the train through a trapdoor in the caboose that only they knew about.

"Normally they are, which is why I thought they would be such a hit and was so eager for them to join the Moscow circus," Vladimir said and covered his ears when he heard supersonic aircraft a short way from them.

"What is that?" Sergei asked. "Who did you call?"

"Oh, no one," Vladimir said. "I suppose the prophecy of the leonine weathervane came true and bad things are going to happen to the city. War has no formal ringmaster."

Women and children cried as they left their husbands and fathers at the train station. Lviv's lions began to depart to take up defensive positions around the city. The time for clowning around had ended. Meanwhile, back on Rynok Square, the weathervane lion dusted himself off and put the carriages back in the Square. After he completed this important task, he climbed back on his perch in the museum wall and muttered to himself that, in time, there would be many more carriages in Rynok Square.

Food for Thought in Pushkin Square

Pushkin Square was a hotspot for demonstrations. It was the first location that a spontaneous protest had taken place during the Cold War, and today in mid-May 2022, another was occurring. The demonstrators were the same usual suspects: the youth, open-minded individuals who did not fully give into the propaganda machine. The war which they were protesting was not cold. It was a hot, live action one. It was the conflict that was taking place in Ukraine some two-hundred-eighty miles away.

"No war. Ukraine is our brother," the protestors cried in unison under the statue of Pushkin, Russia's national poet, in a frock coat.

"If Pushkin were alive, he'd be writing odes lamenting our folly," a young man cried out from the crowd.

As the chanting continued, riot police moved in, beating the protestors with their batons, tasing some of them, and hauling them into white vans to be driven away. The riot police had been working overtime. They had parked their command car across the street. The cars were next to the first McDonald's that had opened in Russia thirty-two years ago. In order to stay awake until the next shift replaced them, they went in small groups to the fast-food restaurant where they purchased coffee.

"Tomorrow, McDonalds will be gone, as they are pulling out of Russia to protest the war," the captain said.

"But the protestors will still be here. That won't change," his deputy said.

"Then what will we buy to keep ourselves awake?" the captain commented as he allowed his coffee to cool. "We all know that McDonald's coffee is the cheapest, and economic times are hard right now. I—'' The captain's response was cut short. He swung at the shins of a protester who had managed to breach makeshift fencing they had put on. The captain struck the intruder with such a force that his knees buckled. He fell to the ground headfirst, gouging his forehead on sharp cobblestone and causing rivers of blood to run into the worn, caulked mortar.

As the protestor struggled to his feet, he said, "You don't really support this war; you would have to be blind to do so. If you are already complaining about the price of coffee, I don't know whether to think you are so short sighted as to only think about the small things in life or if you know how detrimental the war will be to us Russians as well as to the Ukrainians."

"Allow me to enlighten you," the captain said, and he threw his coffee in the protestor's face. Reeling from the shock, the protester took a step backward. He struggled to wipe the contents from his face. He then gave the signal ordering his subordinates to shove the man onto the ground and place him in a headlock so that he could put the full weight of his jackboot on the protestor's neck.

"I am sorry. What was that you were saying about Russia being in the wrong?"

As the man struggled to answer, the captain snapped his fingers and his subordinates hoisted the man up, placed him in plastic handcuffs, and led him away to an idling van.

For the next half hour, the riot police struggled to gain control of the crowd, firing tear gas on several occasions, and the protests slowly began to die down. As the gas cleared from the latest volley that had been fired around noon Moscow time, an enigmatic disheveled figure made his way towards the group. The man, about thirty-five years of age, wore an army uniform which bore the indicative "Z" emblem, the one that the government had adopted as its insignia as a symbol of support for the war in Ukraine.

"Aren't you going to join us, Yevgeny?" asked Oleg, one of the protesters, and Yevgeny's former roommate.

"Or have you not changed since our university days, when you would sit at the back of the class, copy our notes, do well on the exam, and take all the credit?" asked Andrei, another of Yevgeny's old classmates.

"I can't say that I am going to join you," Yevgeny replied. "For I have a higher purpose."

"There you go, being pretentious again," Oleg said as spat on Yevgeny's uniform. "What could be a higher cause than protesting this war, which not only is unjust but will have no benefit for us or Russia for that matter?"

"The Golden Arches," Yevgeny answered. As he spoke, a soldier gestured with an outstretched palm toward the McDonald's which stood across the street from *Izvestiya,* one of Russia's only independent newspapers.

"You look like the Lenin statue by Finland Station with your outstretched hand. What revolution are you spreading?" Oleg asked.

"I'm not the melodramatic one here," Yevgeny snapped. "But you are correct, a revolution is afoot. McDonald's is leaving our homeland, and it is something I can't stomach." Yevgeny continued past his comrades toward the restaurant.

"The real revolution was when they began to censor *Izvestiya* a week ago," Oleg said before starting to chant anti-war slogans. The rest of the protestors followed suit. Yevgeny crossed the street and confronted the riot police.

"Looks like we have a guest just in time for lunch," the leader quipped as he signaled his men to hold their fire. "Hello," he said to the man approaching them, "how did you make it through the protestors?"

"When you have a craving for something as much as I do, anything is possible," Yevgeny said. "But I tell you," Yevgeny stopped walking and stood in front of the riot police, lit a cigarette, and began to smoke with such vengeance that his exhales shrouded his piercing blue eyes.

***

The inside of the 1,087 square meter McDonald's was much like any other McDonald's in a large city. The floors were of colored concrete, the walls of cheap pressed oak ,and the lighting of single iridescent bulbs that were housed in small stage-like lighting fixtures. The primary difference between this McDonald's and others was that it spanned some three floors so as to be able to handle the customer load that came off the streets from one of the world's busiest squares.

Today, however, as had been the case for much of the week, the restaurant was empty save for the riot police who came to purchase coffee. Only one cash register was being manned. One person worked as a cook behind the counter in the "assembly," one of the automated machines that did everything from cook the fries to toast the buns for the sandwiches.

The woman behind the counter was an old woman by the name of Tanya. She was probably old enough to be a pensioner. She resembled a typical babushka who had been taken advantage of by the old soviet system. Missing many teeth, she had long bony hands. Still, when approached by someone who was not part of the police force, she smiled, her white hair bobbing in her cloth bun.

"What can I get you today, young man who is off to defend the motherland?" the woman asked.

"I'll have a chicken sandwich, a hamburger, and a fish sandwich," Yevgeny replied as he plopped his Rubles down in an almost brazen manner. "I hope I have enough money. Why, I barely had enough money for the subway this morning." Yevgeny took his Ruble notes and fondled them between his thumb and forefinger, caressing his thumb on the cheap paper they were printed on as he spoke.

"I will miss this establishment for the food, but I will not miss capitalism or anything else that smacks of the West. And you can skip the fries. If I eat that much, I am not sure I will be able to walk out of here."

"Do you really believe in what Putin says we are fighting for?' The old woman asked as she began to place the food on the man's tray along with the empty cup for him to go fill at the soda fountain.

"Of course," Yevgeny replied. "I didn't have to enlist. The government only recently lowered the minimum age for recruits because of all the losses we have taken."

"But the government says they have been minimal," the old woman replied.

"That's what they say, but we all know the reality," Yevgeny said as he walked over to the soda fountain and helped himself to a Coca Cola while the old woman lifted a fresh batch of fries out of the fryer.

"I don't know," the old woman said. She put two packets of ketchup on the plastic tray. "My father died in The Great Patriotic War, as did two of my brothers. Back then we knew what we were fighting for. Now I just don't know. Well, enjoy your food. I'll be here if you need anything else, but who knows? You might be my last customer."

"If I am still hungry, I will let you know," Yevgeny replied. He proceeded to a table on the third floor where he could not be observed, sat down, said his prayers, and then eyed his first victim, the chicken sandwich.

"How I wish the babushka had not questioned me about my thoughts on the war. Just look at you," Yevgeny said to the chicken sandwich as he unwrapped it from the ubiquitous yellow paper with the even more ubiquitous "M" printed all over it. "You are so beautiful, and you know what they say chickens represent. They are symbols of motherly affection."

As the man spoke, he thought of his own mother. She had asked him why he had asked for subway fare that morning, as his work at a local high-tech firm was only two blocks away from the flat he shared with her, his father, and his fiancée. He told her he was going to Pushkin Square.

"Come back alive," she said. "God knows what is happening to the protestors."

"Mama will probably be calling the local precinct when I do not return," Yevgeny commented to the sandwich. "Little will she know that I will be on a train on the way to the front and may very well be coming back in a body bag. Yevgeny raised the chicken sandwich to his mouth.

He was halfway to starting what he thought would be a pleasant meal when the bun began to shake violently in his hands, causing him to drop the sandwich. As the chicken began its descent to the floor, the wilted, watery lettuce, the type that you only see in a fast-food restaurant, arced up and threw the top of the bun off. It secured itself to the meat of the sandwich. The leaf of lettuce then folded itself in half to make a pair of wings, just before the remainder of the sandwich hit the floor and carried it aloft. Stunned, Yevgeny watched in amazement as the sandwich flew across the room and down the stairs. He was about to pursue his food when he looked up at the closed-circuit television, only to notice on a camera that the chicken had flown out of the drive-through window into the lap of a passenger, whose shriek was nearly inaudible to the man, but her surprise was not. She drove off without paying for her order, leaving the babushka with a cone of rapidly melting ice cream in her hands.

Yevgeny panted in anxiety and began to take deep breaths in an effort to tame his adrenaline when the babushka came running up the stairs.

"What happened?!" she asked.

"I don't know," Yevgeny exclaimed. "I was just about to enjoy my sandwich when..."

"It sprouted wings and flew," the babushka finished his sentence. She grabbed the cleaning cart and mopped up the mayonnaise from the floor. "I hope you leave a gratuity as you are driving away our last customers. While I know it is not customary to do so at McDonald's, I hope you consider," the babushka said. She put her hands on her hips and addled down the steps like either a proud peacock or a portly old duck, the type of bird she was trying to be the man simply could not decipher given the circumstances of what had just happened.

Once the babushka was out of sight, Yevgeny turned to the fish sandwich.

"Did you feel like me initially?" Yevgeny asked the fish sandwich he held in his hands. "Did you initially doubt your higher purpose in life, or should I say in your case death when you were caught in icy waters off Alaska? Did you see your purpose as to be like the fish in the Gospels to feed the people of Russia who had been shut out for the rest of the world who had been denied the word of God?" As Yevgeny spoke, the fish sandwich began to squirm in his hands. It continued to do so until it had turned a full one hundred eighty degrees and then began a jerking motion toward the bucket of water. The mop was still on the floor next to Yevgeny's table.

"You want to return to the water already?" Yevgeny asked the sandwich. "Am I not worthy to receive you? Don't worry, I promise you my intent is sincere. My intent is to pursue you in the West, as that is why I am fighting, to have access to McDonald's again," Yevgeny said. The fish sandwich continued to squirm until it finally freed itself and fell into the bucket of water. It began to swim in circles; the breading from its patty shape dissolved quickly, leaving the white, boneless flesh to fend for itself in the water.

As Yevgeny was processing this scene, the babushka came up to retrieve her mop. When she saw the scene in the bucket, the babushka looked up. "Do you have to cause such chaos? This restaurant is my sanctuary from what is going on outside!"

"Of course, it is!" Yevgeny snapped. "It is telling me how desperate it is to have me follow them. It cannot bear to fathom the idea that it is being exiled from here, when it, one of the most emblematic symbols of capitalism, gave people like us opportunities. What did it do to deserve this? The West complains of how many people have been displaced in Ukraine due to the war." Yevgeny gestured toward the stairs to the drive-through window and then to the bucket in which the fish sandwich was swimming in concentric circles. "Well, look at what the West is creating. It is even making our food be displaced."

"They say that an army marches on its stomach and well, it does not look like this food is very well disposed to fill you up before you catch your train," the babushka said.

"Leave me alone!" Yevgeny snapped. He banged his fist on the table. Some of the Coca Cola breached the rim of the paper cup and spilled on the hamburger. The babushka made herself scarce, and Yevgeny turned his attention to the hamburger.

"The Golden Calf," Yevgeny exclaimed. He held the double patty between his forefinger and thumb of his left hand, and he caressed the two patties which hung over the bun like a bloodhound's tongue with his right. "If there is anything that is emblematic of McDonald's, it is you. Surely you can understand why I am willingly going to war. Why, I would lay down my life for you." Yevgeny paused as he looked around him to make sure he was still alone, that the prying babushka had not returned to either admonish him or to try to convince him that his logic for backing Russia's incursion into Ukraine was flawed before he spoke to the hamburger again. "In fact, I am debating whether or not I should consume you so as to prove my devotion to you and the institution that birthed you," Yevgeny said as he put the hamburger down and thought for a moment. But this moment was one moment too many. As soon as he released the sandwich from his grasp, it sprouted a pair of legs, jumped off the table, and ran down the stairs mooing.

"Wait, come back!" Yevgeny cried as he gave chase. Upon rounding the landing, he caught sight of the counter where the babushka was filling an order for the leader of the riot police, who had ordered a batch of hamburgers. The running sandwich gave another *moo*, which prompted the hamburgers on the tray to sprout legs and follow Yevgeny's burger toward the door.

Yevgeny's sandwich waited for the others to catch up. Yevgeny raced to the entrance doors and exclaimed "It is yet another sign that the food thinks the war is just, as these hamburgers are following me. Come," Yevgeny said to the burgers, "It is time to catch our train." Yevgeny opened the door and ran down the street toward the subway that would take him to the train station, the burgers following in hot pursuit.

"Perhaps it is because they want to flee Russia because they are disgusted by the conflict," the babushka called after Yevgeny, before the door slammed shut by a harsh gust of wind.

For the next six hours, the babushka watched out the window. Oleg and Andrei were the last of the protestors to be bundled up and tossed in the waiting vans like bales of hay on a farm. No other customers came, and finally she put up the closed sign.

She mopped the floor muttering to herself, "If the very substance that sustains us, food, is against the war, that should tell us something. We Russians are gluttons for punishment." As she said these words, the remaining remnants of the fish sandwich leapt out of the bucket, did a somersault, and dove back into the fetid water.

An Octopus in Cordoba

In the heart of Cordoba, sat a house with a luxurious bedroom. Across the bed, adorned with gold-laced Egyptian cotton sheets, stood a massive aquarium. Along the tank's bottom was the coarsest sand that had been imported from the coast of Oregon. An artificial dark brown, almost vulgar rocky outcrop was huddled against the side of the tank

The resident of this tank was a female salmon-colored *Giant Pacific Octopus*, with two gills and a trinity of hearts within. Attached to this oval-like sphere were eight tentacles lined with thousands of chestnut-colored suction cups, having more taste receptors than the human tongue. The tentacles wandered about the tank looking for food, acting autonomously from one another and the rest of her as a whole.

Their quixotic search was in vain since she had just laid her eggs. If nature was to have its way, the octopus would not eat anymore. She would retreat to her den, guard the eggs from predators, and die before the offspring hatched. In time, the octopus would turn a ghastly white and become emaciated. Her torso would wrinkle and resemble the flayed skin of St. Bartholomew in Michelangelo's *The Last Judgment.* Her tentacles would become limp shadows of their strong proud selves.

Her mate was nowhere to be found. Even if the tank had been large enough to house two gargantuan cephalopods, it would not have made a difference. Once they had spread their seed, the males went on their own way, continuing to propagate without any parental responsibility.

Along with the octopus tank and the bed, the entire room was graced by luxury. On either side of the bed were two marble nightstands upon which were golden vases adorned with inscriptions from the Quran. They were bought by the owner's late husband, a wealthy banker from one of Spain's oldest entrepreneurial families. Both husband and wife had lived for luxury, but now, luxury meant very little to The Widow.

Above the bed hung a large golden crucifix and an iron chandelier. The walls were a perfect replica of the arches in the famous mosque-cathedral of Cordoba, and Turkish carpets covered the marble floor.

Past the doorway, opposite the one leading to the patio, was a small kitchen with a coral-colored backsplash with a herringbone pattern. There was the dining room with an oak table, and on a wall hung a tapestry, one depicting a copy of the painting of *Auto-da-fe on Plaza Mayor Madrid* by Rizi. Here The Widow often took her suppers alone, contemplating why she had stayed in her loveless marriage to a husband who was constantly away and had refused to grant her what she had wanted most—children of her own.

"Look at what I have bought to celebrate our fiftieth wedding anniversary," the banker had said to his wife only a week ago, a week before his death. "It is a symbol of how our marriage has grown. You see, all those tentacles are autonomous; they have their own agendas. We have managed to be married while having our own lives, too."

Yes, like you are always away and never there for me. And when it shoots out its ink, it is indicative of how you prefer to be alone, unseen by the one you should be with.

After the funeral, her husband's colleagues, business associates, friends, and family gathered to reflect on his life. The comments from the guests had not been ones of sympathy, rather they only lauded his philanthropy and praised what they saw as her husband providing a life of luxury.

That evening The Widow sat on the patio surrounded by flowers which grew from pots that were anchored in the white stucco walls. She intended to lay some of the flowers on her husband's grave so as to pay lip service to societal norms. She fondled her pearl necklace and walked into her bedroom past the tank. She saw the octopus guarding the plethora of pearl-like eggs near the rocky outcrop.

"What am I going to do with you?" The Widow asked. "You embody everything I want, and what is ironic is that should nature take its course, you will die after you complete your mission. At least your life has a purpose. What am I to do now that I am a widow? I resented my husband greatly, but I still lived with him and put up with him, all to keep up appearances. Such is life," The Widow said as she put down her cigarette and signed the cross while muttering her prayers to an icon of The Virgin Mary that hung on the wall.

***

The Widow entered the Church of San Pedro where she and her late husband were parishioners. She'd been a devout Catholic all her life. Her observance grew after her marriage as the liturgy comforted her as her husband became withdrawn. After Mass, she spoke with The Priest.

"Still grieving?" The Priest asked as he put a paternal hand on The Widow's shoulder.

"No," The Widow whispered. "I'm hurt."

"After fifty years, half a century?" The priest said.

"Of sadness," The Widow finished the priest's sentence. "He always told me that his greatest legacy in our marriage was his ability to allow us to remain as individuals. He never spent any time with me, and the time I had to myself, he enlisted me into helping him in superfluous activities."

"Such as?" the priest inquired.

"Well, digging through the baptismal records to find out about his illustrious pedigree, for one thing," The Widow said.

"Were you ever curious—" the priest began.

"About mine?" The Widow said. "Of course, I am."

"Well," the priest led The Widow to his study. "You are welcome to see the records, everything should be here" the priest opened a drawer in which the records were stored.

The Widow began to look through the records. While browsing, she found that her grandparents were not natives of Andalusia but that they had come from Lisbon, Portugal.

"I always thought that my family had been in Cordoba for at least twelve generations," The Widow remarked. "I don't see anything before 1780."

"I do know anything else either," the priest said. "But I have sent other people in your shoes to the rabbi with whom I lead interfaith dialogues. He has been able to help."

"Why would a rabbi be of any use?" The Widow asked.

The priest remained mute and continued cleaning a chalice.

The Widow rose from the desk curtsied to the priest and left the church. The walk to the synagogue was only a stone's throw away, a third of a mile at most. Nevertheless, it was perplexing. Cordoba, with its layers of history built on top of each other, was like an unfinished wedding cake. The different religions in the city had co-existed throughout history, but in some epochs, they had fought and been vindictive, as demonstrated in the architecture of the Mosque-Cathedral. The building was originally a church built on a Visigoth shrine which then became a mosque and then a church again.

The Widow walked down the narrow streets of the Jewish quarter passing the patios in front of the houses that had been the inspiration for her own. She passed the statute of Moses Maimonides, the philosopher

The Widow pushed the door open. She found the main sanctuary empty. In front of the rows of chairs was a table with prayer books that were still open. The ark was made of simple pine and the plaster work, with geometric shapes on either side, reminiscent of the architecture in the city's mosque. On the lectern a book entitled *The Guide of the Perplexed* by Moses Maimonides caught The Widow's eye.

"Hello?" The Widow called out. She waited for a response, then just as she was about to leave, she heard a voice behind her.

"I am sorry for not coming earlier. I was in the basement," a lanky balding man with long bony hands said. He was wearing a head covering, long black pants, and a pressed white shirt. He looked to be in his nineties. "What brings you here? I have not seen you before."

"Yes, Ra, Rab- "The Widow began.

"Rabbi," the man finished The Widow's struggled sentence. "Pleased to meet you."

"And you as well. I was sent here by my priest who advised me that I might find out more about my family heritage."

"You are not the only one who has come here from your church," The rabbi said as he opened the ark and removed a small wooden chest with discolored copper fastenings. "What is your surname?"

"Gonzalez, no, Hernandez," The Widow corrected herself, remembering the pain her husband had inflicted upon her by usurping her identity with their marriage.

"Hernandez. Hernandez," The rabbi mumbled as he thumbed through several index cards. "Were people like you not interested, these cards would have been thrown out."

"May I make a copy of the cards?" The Widow asked.

"Of course. I will make one for you." The rabbi went to the back of the shul and made copies upon returning he said, "Most of the Jews who stayed converted to Catholicism and entirely shed their and heritage within a generation or two. Some of The Grand Inquisitors, including the infamous Torquemada, were of Jewish descent. People like him were so eager to reap the rewards of the Reconquista, so they sold their own out."

The Widow raised her eyebrows as the rabbi spoke. She had read about the Spanish Inquisition and many of its horrors, but she had not known about all those who derived rewards from it.

"I also wanted to give you this, which I give to any visitor to the synagogue," the rabbi handed The Widow a book. "This is *The Guide of the Perplexed,* by Maimonides, Cordoba's most famous Jewish son, I am sure you passed his statue on the way here."

"I did pass it. Thank you, I will be sure to read it," The Widow said.

The Widow leafed through *The Guide of the Perplexed*, on her way home. Most of the work was far too dense, and boring, but a part about the levels of charity caught her eye.

About a third of the way through, his treatise Maimonides laid out the eight levels of charity in terms of altruism. "Eight. Why does that number disturb me?" The Widow said as she stopped at a tapas bar and placed a to-go order for a large plate of octopus cheese, and olives.

When The Widow got home, she put *The Guide of the Perplexed* on her bed. She then walked to the kitchen, plated her meal, and walked to the octopus's tank. Aside from a lone tentacle that was hanging over the entrance to the den, the octopus was nowhere to be seen. Nature was taking its course, and it had retreated into its abode protect its eggs from the outside world.

"Sometimes, I wish it was you on this plate," The Widow said, rapping on the tank. After this, she ate dinner, said grace, and sat down across from the tapestry.

The tapestry had been an acquisition of her husband. It was yet another reminder of how he controlled her. It made her grimace, its image depicted the trials of the Jews who had not embraced Christianly. But The Widow took comfort that now the priest and rabbi of the town held interfaith dialogues. After she finished her dinner, she picked up *The Guide of the Perplexed.*

"*The eighth rung of charity is to give to the poor grudgingly,*" The Widow read aloud. "An example is giving to a beggar while telling him to stop being lazy and to get a job," she said.

"*The seventh rung is to give less than one should when asked.* This would have fit my husband when we were married. The phone was constantly ringing off the hook from people soliciting donations to this museum, to that charity. While he always gave, it was pocket change."

"*The sixth rung is to give without being asked,*" The Widow chuckled. "My late husband would never do this. She looked down at the book again. *The fifth level states that one gives directly to the poor without being asked by putting something in their hand.*"

As The Widow moved to turn the page, she caught sight of the octopus. It was fully out of its den and had arranged its tentacles under its bulbous head so that it resembled a dog resting its head on its front paws as it starred at The Widow.

"Listening, are we?" The Widow said. "We advance up to the fourth rung. *The giver knows the recipient of the charity, but the recipient does not know who the giver is.*" The Widow took a bite of cheese before continuing to read. "To the upper rungs. *The third rung is where the recipient does not know his benefactor, but the donor knows to whom he gives.*"

As The Widow read the octopus began to scale the wall of the tank with its tentacles. "I can see I am piquing your interest," The Widow said. "Onto the highest two levels. An example of this would be one putting used clothes in a box on a street anonymously and allowing the poor to come collect when one is not present. Onto the highest rung. *The giver enters into a partnership with the poor to help them find employment, so they do not need to be dependent on others.*"

"Don't you worry," The Widow began. She shook her cigarette holder in the direction of the tank, much like how a disciplinary teacher might shake her ruler at an unruly student. "I did my homework; I know that within four months your young should hatch. I cannot let you succeed where I failed, I cannot let you become a mother. To hear my late husband's associates, sing his praises was hard enough, and seeing you is not making things any easier."

As she said this, the octopus curled up and retreated into its den leaving a cloud of ink behind.

"I am not sure you are shooting that ink to taunt me as if to say that I will never come up with a way to coax you to go against nature, or to say you are afraid." The Widow doused her cigarette, then turned to the icon of the Virgin Mary. She said her prayers and drifted off to sleep. She dreamt about how she would deal with the octopus that her late husband had saddled her with.

***

The next day was beautiful and sunny, with a light breeze. Before leaving the house, The Widow left *The Guide of the Perplexed* on the page of charity facing the tank.

She then went to the gardens of the Alcázar de los Reyes. While listening to the sounds of the fountains and admiring the flowers, The Widow hatched her plan. She went to the library where she poured over every book and manuscript on octopuses that she could find. After this, she went to the market to buy groceries. This was an essential step, as she planned to use food to manipulate the octopus into following the levels of Maimonides charity so that she would become an unfit mother.

Upon getting home she saw the octopus hunched behind *The Guide of the Perplexed.* The octopus moved one of its tentacles across the pages as if trying to turn them.

“What a pleasant surprise, ” The Widow said. “It is as if you sense that I am going to make use of this book in my dealings with you. I spent the entire day learning about you, and I know your tentacles have free will, and that you have nine brains and three hearts.”

The Widow went to the fridge and got out a shrimp. She scaled the step ladder next to the tank and dropped it gingerly. She climbed down to watch the octopus. At first nothing happened, the shrimp spun around in circles, carried by the currents of the filters. But then as the smell of the carrion began to permeate the water, a tentacle began to slowly migrate toward the shrimp.

As it approached the shrimp, the tentacle hovered around the shellfish, as if attempting to pick the opportune moment to strike. Finally, the tentacle made its move and grasped the tail of the shrimp, disconnecting it from the body.

The journey across to the den was slow. It seemed as if the tentacle was moving as slowly as possible. When it reached the den, it made several "false" entrances before retracting with the shrimp. Finally, it deposited the contents in the beak of the octopus who ate it excitedly.

"The eighth rung of charity, where the donor gives grudgingly when asked. Very good, very good," The Widow said. "Let's see if we can go on to our next lesson," The Widow returned to the refrigerator and took out a sliver of cod and put it in the tank. "I will ask on your behalf: Please give me something to eat," The Widow said. "Remember, our goal is to follow Maimonides' levels of charity in ascending order."

The second attempt to adhere to the rungs of charity began much like he first. The cod floating around in limbo for five minutes until a different tentacle emerged from the den. Moving at the same speed as the first, it hesitated less to grab the piece of fish. The journey back to the den was faster than the first tentacle and The Widow was even able to see the octopus poke her head out and consume the piece of food.

"Very good, very good," The Widow said. She then got up off the bed, made dinner, washed the dishes, and took some time on the patio.

She watched the flowers close for the night and shed a tear. They reminded her of how she would wait up for her husband late in the evenings, waiting for the phone call which he always said he would make after he clutched a money-making deal over a dinner. Then she would finally fall asleep, having not heard from him. That night, The Widow repeated this ritual, only retiring for the evening until the last flower had closed up.

***

The Widow decided to continue her plan with the octopus every two weeks. In between feedings, she tried to rationalize her actions. First, The Widow told the rabbi of her exploits, albeit a highly censored version.

"Did you find anything out about your family?" the rabbi asked.

"No, nothing really. You were right, there were many Jews who took the surname Hernandez upon formally converting."

"I thought so," the rabbi shook his head.

"But I found the book you gave me interesting," The Widow said.

"Really? I am intrigued," the rabbi said. "Tell me more."

"Well, I have this octopus, that I am trying to manipulate—"

"An octopus?" the rabbi interjected.

"Yes, an octopus, that was given to me as a pet by my late husband, and I am doing so via the levels of charity. The idea came to me as it has eight arms, and *The Guide of the Perplexed* expounds upon eight levels of charity.

"That seems charitable indeed," the rabbi said. "I am glad that you have been able to make use of the *Guide of the Perplexed*.

The Widow was more honest, about her exploits, with the priest.

"Tell me more about this octopus of yours," the priest said.

"My plan is quite simple. If I allow nature to take its course, the octopus will guard its eggs and die of starvation just before they hatch. However, I will keep it alive until its children hatch. Then, I will stop feeding it so that it will grow so hungry that it will cannibalize its own young."

"How dreadful," the priest said. "There must be something that is immensely bothering you which drives you to do this."

"That creature was a gift from my husband. It has laid eggs. I always wanted children, you have known that for forty years," The Widow wrung her hands. "In spite of all our praying, all your couple's counseling, and your Masses, nothing bore fruit to change his mind. This cruelty that he has saddled me with from beyond the grave is a cross that is too much to bear."

"But that is not a reason to take out your feelings on an innocent creature," the priest said.

"I know I know," The Widow wailed. "But I cannot help myself. There must be a way I can continue with my plan."

"You have free will. I hope you are able to find peace in another way," the priest said.

"As do I," The Widow then covered her face with her black shawls and left the church. On the way home, she purchased more seafood.

The Widow stared at the octopus. It was back in its den, save one tentacle that was hanging out of the entrance. The tentacle was in a circular shape with the suction cups facing outward. The tentacle moved in a circular spiral-like motion so that the suction cups went round and round in the same circle. The motion reminded The Widow of rosary beads falling as she prayed the rosary often.

"I take it that you think that you are holier than I am," The Widow said as she rapped on the tank. The tentacle retreated into its den. "The sixth rung is to give adequately when being asked, and I can see that you are hungry," The Widow said, placing some squid in the tank. The tentacle accepted the offering with gusto and took it back to its den where the octopus's mouth received it.

The Widow watched and said, "Rung five, the highest of the lower rungs is to give without being asked. Let's see how smart you are." The Widow left another piece of squid above the tank on a ledge, after which she went to bed.

***

In the morning, The Widow awoke to a loud slam. Startled, she observed the octopus trying to lift the lid off the tank so as to get the squid. After three tries, it succeeded. A tentacle eagerly reached for the food. It appeared so zealous, and it seemed as if the rest of the creature did not notice that food had been dropped in the tank. It gave before being asked.

"Excellent," The Widow said. "Everything is going as planned. Now to the higher rungs. We will start tonight."

That morning, she left the house in a better mood. She attended Mass for the first time since her husband's death with a smile on her face, still she was conflicted about her actions vis-a-vis the octopus.

"The fourth rung," The Widow said when she came home. "Is where the recipient does not know the donor. To make this work," The Widow rapped on the tank again, "I need cooperation from you and your tentacles."

The Widow rapped on the tank a third and fourth time, each time she rapped with more force, until the octopus became frightened and released a cloud of ink. Within minutes the entire tank was so black that The Widow could not see anything, neither could the octopus. The Widow put a piece of flounder in the tank but held it in her hand. She waited patiently until a tentacle came and snatched the flounder from her and gave it to the octopus, who remained in her den.

"Good we completed the fourth rung as you do not directly know the donor, *me*, as one of your tentacles was the intermediary. Onto the third rung where the donor knows the recipient, but the latter does not know his benefactor."

The Widow put some more flounder in the tank and waited. Again, within a few minutes another tentacle came and took the food before traveling back through the sea of ink to the den.

"Superb, your tentacle fed you but you, but you do not know which one," The Widow said. Once the ink cleared, she was surprised to see the cephalopod entirely out of its den. It swam around the tank, looking for food for fifteen minutes.

"Looking for food, and more importantly, leaving your children!" The Widow exclaimed, "You will become a mother, but the question is do I execute the final stage of my plan?"

The Widow then went to the patio and spent the rest of the day tending to the flora. She was conflicted. She resented the octopus, and at the same time she also felt guilty for taking her anger out on it.

That evening The Widow went out to eat, a first since her husband died. Before going to sleep, she took time to admire the preparations for Fiesta de La Cross. There were crosses made from plants and flowers paraded on the streets.

As she slept, the octopus, full of life, wandered the tank in search of food, like an errant Don Quixote.

***

The Widow was determined to keep her plan, but she could not think of a way to execute the second highest rung of charity, where neither the donor nor recipient know each other. Furthermore, her conscience was bothering her. What would happen to the octopus after its young hatched, and she stopped feeding it? After it ate the children, would she then let it starve?

"What am I going to do? The Widow said. "Maybe I should just let you starve and act as if I had not embarked on this enterprise. Let's say nothing happened and let nature take its course.

As The Widow spoke, she could hear splashes, followed by a thud as the top of the tank fell. The Widow retrieved the hood and scaled the step ladder to put it back. As she lowered it back on, a tentacle hoisted itself up and grabbed her free hand.

"Let go! Let go!" The Widow cried as she struggled to free herself, but the octopus was relentless. A struggle ensued until the offending tentacle placed something slimy in her hand. The Widow dropped the hood onto the floor. Cursing, she climbed down the ladder glancing at the contents in her hand. It took her a few minutes to discern what was in it.

Walking out on the patio The Widow saw that she was holding a glob of octopus eggs. The eggs were developed enough that she was able to see the embryos of baby octopuses swimming in their shiny sacs.

The Widow returned to her bedroom and climbed up the ladder and released the eggs back into the tank. "You completed rung two," she said to the octopus, "as your young do not know me, and I do not know them. But I am the recipient, for if you allow me, I will benefit from the life you have borne. As you know, the highest level is the gift of partnership. I feel that I finally know who I am and where I belong."

The two mothers looked at each other. Together they had climbed the ladder of charity. The octopus turned from a dark shade of pink to cloudy blue, and The Widow smiled.

Beethoven's Butterflies

There were two events in Chaing's life that had happened unexpectedly. First, he had just moved to Taipei from the countryside to take a mundane job at the *Su Ho Paper Museum*. Later, he would also fall in love at first sight.

Chaing did not like his new vocation as both a docent in the museum and a worker in the old-fashioned mill. He considered the menial work beneath him, as he had trained as an environmental attorney and had only recently been laid off. His only solace from the mill's constant smell of sulfides and ammonia was the paycheck he took home.

After a while, however, Chaing became interested in all the types of paper he created and worked with and even took up origami in the small room on the top floor of the museum. It was during one of these lunches about a week after the start of his employment that he was introduced to one of the more unusual aspects of Taiwanese life: the way the Taipei collected and disposed of its waste. The garbage and recycling trucks blared out Beethoven's *Für Elise* and *Any Empty Wine Bottles for Sale,* respectively.

Chaing had spent the last half hour of his lunch break folding paper cranes, trying to make a thousand, which according to Japanese belief would bring one good fortune. He was on his fiftieth crane—many others had already gone into the recycling bin as they were imperfect—when he heard music being played from a microphone mounted on a garbage truck. It was followed by the popular song from the recycling truck which drove behind. This ritual could be heard several times a day pumped out from the loudspeakers at such a volume that it could be heard three blocks away.

Chaing was putting the recycling bin outside when his boss reprimanded him. "In Taipei we hand deliver our waste to the drivers when they come. It is forbidden to leave your bin on the street."

Once outside, Chaing noticed that people lined up even if their trash bins were not full. He took notice of what others threw away. Most items were mundane, banana peels to broken down cardboard boxes. Chaing listened as people gossiped about topics ranging from the latest baseball scores to international politics. One item, and the young woman holding it, caught Chaing's eye. Attractive with doe-shaped eyes and an oval face, she was wearing white cotton shorts and a tank top. In her long lithe hands, she held what looked like wires, glistening in the sun.

"They are violin strings that snapped," the young woman explained to Chaing when she noticed him staring at her. "Whenever someone new sees me, they always stare." She handed the strings to the garbage collector who unceremoniously tossed them into the truck as it played a crescendo in Beethoven's piece. They both watched the cords being devoured.

"I wonder how Beethoven would feel about you learning his renowned piece from a garbage truck," Chaing said.

"Who knows, but I am sure he broke more than one string in his time. Besides, they say music is good at making plants grow, and I do work at the botanical gardens," the young woman said, smiling as she walked away down the street.

Chaing was enamored and followed her from a safe distance so she would not notice. Electricity and excitement were pumping through his body like one of Beethoven's scores as it built up to a crescendo. He ducked into *Tealicious Bubble Cafe* across from the gardens so he could view her and not to arouse any suspicion.

***

"You are late," Chaing's boss snapped upon his return.

Chaing had been so swept up, so hyper focused on the new woman of his desire, that he brushed off his boss's harsh reprimand when he came back to the factory.

"I know," Chaing said. "It's my fault. Feel free to dock my wages."

From then on, Chaing spent his lunch breaks at the *Tealisicous Bubble Cafe*. There, he could observe the young woman playing her violin in the garden, playing the same tune, "Für Elise."

The cafe became Chaing's observation outpost, where under the guise of reading a book about butterflies—which were the most commonly created objects by tourists who folded origami at the paper museum—he observed the woman. He tried to learn her habits: what she ate for lunch on her break; how she judged her music playing abilities; her frowns, smiles, and occasional scowls. These observations went on for two weeks before Chaing got up the nerve to say something to her.

"You must really be a fan of Beethoven," Chaing said one day upon venturing into the garden, ostensibly to look at the rose bushes, whose buds had yet to open.

"No, it is just easier to learn when you hear the garbage trucks passing all day," the girl said. "I just started practicing the violin a month ago. Besides, my name is Elise as well. I was given it as my parent's favorite composer is Beethoven."

"Well, you are quite talented," Chaing said before he had to catch the bus to work on time.

Back at the museum, Chaing busied himself beating the paper fibers, bleaching them, and cutting them down to size. As often happens when one is freshly in love, everything, even the boring task of working at the papermill had a new shiny varnish of happiness. Now, the fibers did not smell, the tours of the museum Chaing led were not so tedious, even if he gave the same explanations a dozen times a day. Chaing made use of the various papers at hand to create a beautiful sheen of red that matched the buds of the roses that would bloom in the garden later that month. He then graphed onto it the golden score depicting Beethoven's "Für Elise," as well a proposal of marriage in silver lettering.

Like a butterfly developing in its chrysalis, Chaing slowly built up the courage to continue pursuing Elise. On his next visit to *Tealicious*, Chaing noticed actual live butterflies over Elise's head as she practiced her violin in the gardens. He tried to research them in his guidebook, but they were moving too quickly for him to identify. Chaing watched her brush away the fluttering insects with her bow, and he gathered himself up and crossed the street toward woman he loved.

"Are they bothering you?" Chaing asked.

"They are. But there is not much I can do about them. They are protected by the law here. And besides, they are so pretty." Elise pointed at the butterfly book Chaing was carrying.

"I can see you think highly of them, too," she said.

"I agree. They are beautiful," Chaing said. "Judging by the six different sized spots they have on their orange wings they appear to be Peacock Pansies. I love how the spots go from small to large as they work their way up their wings."

"Yes, but it will only get harder to practice as when the season goes on, when the flowers start to bloom there will be more. I love giving tours of the gardens and showing them to people but I can't say they help my violin playing."

"If only there was a way that they could focus on something else," Chaing said, but he had to run for his bus. "Goodbye," he said, waving and smiling.

"Take care. Safe travels," Elise called after him.

The bus drove by the tree-lined back roads. Chaing looked at the window and saw sagging trees laden with butterfly chrysalises preparing to hatch and his mind began to swirl with ideas. He knew what he had to do.

Chaing spent the next week after work making a dozen more paper flowers. One humid Monday, he took off from work and set out early to the *Tealisicous Bubble Cafe*, carrying his flowers. He tried to keep his adrenaline in check. *Tealisicous* was packed with people, all following the custom of sharing tables with strangers when seating was scarce. Three walls of bamboo surrounded the tea shop, and its cheap white plastic chairs were in complete contrast to the sophisticated drinks that were served. A few fans hanging from the white canvas ceiling droned like crickets. The only available half-vacant table was near the curb where Chaing came face to face with the lone silhouette of a man who appeared translucent and ghost-like.

Chaing sat down and observed that the diaphanous man had an eerie resemblance to an individual renowned for nearly two hundred years. The man was pouring over notebooks, writing with a quill. When Chaing got closer, he could see that the notebooks were filled with unevenly cut parchment, yellowed with age, and were not unlike the acid-free high-quality paper Chaing made. Their covers were of worn leather and the silk tassels which could be tied to keep them shut were frayed at the edges. The notebooks were sprawled out all over the table, barely giving Chaing room to put down his cup of tea. Chaing noticed that the notebooks seemed to be filled with musical scores, the signature Ludwig Van Beethoven in the right-hand corner. The ghostly man, hunched over in a frock coat and wearing a red vest with golden buttons, had wild silvery unkempt hair that reminded Chiang of the medusa's hair he had seen depicted on Greek Vases at the National Museum in Taipei the previous weekend.

"Hello," Chaing said as politely as he could. "Hello?" he said, but again no answer.

Then as Chaing sipped his tea, a trio of butterflies glided in and hovered over the café. They were still damp from having just hatched from their chrysalises. Mistaking the paper umbrellas that adorned each cup of tea for real flowers, the butterflies flew closer. One of them landed delicately on the cup of the ghost who, Chaing felt, could only be Beethoven himself. The famous composer brushed his hand through the air and, in doing so, spilled his tea over his precious notebook.

"Scheisee," the man with wild hair bellowed. He grabbed some napkins and sopped up the mess. When the filth was cleaned the man said: "Danke."

"You are welcome," said Chaing and then proceeded to put his flowers to the side so the notebooks could be quickly moved away from the damp area of the table.

Chaing knew that the great composer had grown deaf in his later years, and that except for his most intimate friends, he rarely spoke, instead using writing as his primary form of communication. Eager to communicate with such a titan of music, Chaing took one of his flowers, unfolded it, took a pen from his pocket, and on the side where he had not copied the score to "Für Elise," he wrote:

I am sorry about what happened to your notebooks.

Chaing gently maneuvered the former flower toward the composer. The composer wrote back: *I appreciate your sympathy. But I already am going to have to throw out some of my scores.* Beethoven broke off his writing and looked up at Chaing before continuing.

Tell me, is that a copy of my piece "Für Elise" that I see amidst the folds in your paper flowers?

Yes, it is, Chaing wrote back.

Beethoven pulled a bottle of wine from his frock coat and poured himself some into an empty teacup. He then reached over and dumped Chaing's remaining tea on the floor before filling his glass as well.

So apparently the garbage trucks aren't the only thing that plagiarized my score here. Others make use of it too.

I suppose.

Beethoven put his hand on Chaing and smiled. *I trust you know that I wrote that piece for an unrequited love of mine.*

Yes, but I am hoping my use of your work will have different results. I hope you do not take offense to my using it.

Beethoven mustered a smile. He took a swing of wine and wrote quickly.

No, I take offense to refuse vehicles making use of one of my many masterpieces, and to add insult to injury the truck that comes behind it collects glass and plastic. I am told it plays a silly tune that shouldn't even be heard in the same century as mine. Is the afterlife trying to get me to give up the only pleasure I still have in death—drinking? None of the music I write now will ever be played again. Even the butterflies are making a mockery out of my music.

Just then, another butterfly landed on Chaing's cup, but unlike Beethoven, Chaing did not shoo it away. He watched as the newly hatched insect pulled the two halves of its proboscises together to form a drinking straw, necessary for it to be able to feed on the pollen that sustained it. Chaing needed to share this understanding with the great composer.

They feel pain like us.

Beethoven put down his cup of wine.

I beg your pardon?

Butterflies, when they hatch, have to pull their probiscis together in a painful process.

Beethoven ignored Chaing, pushed the notebook away and spoke aloud. "Who are those origami flowers for, anyway?"

Chaing wrote in response. *They are for a beautiful girl who plays her violin in the botanical gardens. I am in love with her, and I am proposing to her.*

Chaing pointed discretely to his true love who had just come outside. She took out her violin, and as always began to play "Für Elise."

Beethoven looked up at Elise.

"I must admit, she is attractive. If I were alive and, in your shoes, I might be inclined to make her one of my conquests as well," Beethoven said.

Chaing grew more excited and wrote as quickly as he could. *Her name is Elise. That is why I have attached my proposition on flowers that bear your score.*

"A little unconventional for my taste, but I do wish you luck."

Beethoven got up but before he left said, "Let me know how it goes. I'll be at the wine bar across from the Sun Yat-sen Memorial tonight. If I see you there, I will assume you have come to drink your sorrows away with me and cry on my shoulder."

***

Chaing put down his teacup and crossed the street to the gardens. He walked past the first rose bush and surveyed the rosebuds which were red and soft, just as he imagined were Elise's lips. The nascent flowers nestled against the iron-wrought gates, ivy growing in between. Around their bases were patches of soft ferns from the bushes to form a path to the greenhouse. Chaing looked for the perfect cluster of red rose buds to hide his delicate creations, just the right spot that would look natural. He busied himself placing his paper flowers, trying to angle them so that the gold leaf caught the rays of the sun and so Elise would see them right away. Elise watched, then she stopped playing her violin. At first, she tried to look as if she were not interested, but after a few minutes she became curious and walked over to him.

"Trying to attract the butterflies?" Elise asked.

"Well, a certain one," Chaing replied, his face turning red.

"I think it is cruel to make them use their precious energy and believe there is pollen in your flowers where they are just paper."

Still, Elise put her violin in its case and plucked a paper flower from between the thorns. As Elsie read the note, the iconic sound from the local garbage truck could be heard down the block. It was time for the noon garbage collection. When the truck arrived, Elise walked to the curb and extended Chaing's lovely paper flowers to the man who tossed them into the recycling compactor.

He felt like a butterfly that had just been captured by an insect collector and placed in a chloroform jar to die. Now, even the most basic tasks like breathing seemed herculean in nature.

"You are not the first who has asked me to marry him since I started playing the violin and I am sure you will not be the last. In either case, I am spoken for."

Elise turned her back on Chaing and went back to playing her violin trying to match the exact musical measure heard from the street. The butterflies finding no pollen in Chaing's paper flowers, flew away.

Chaing's heart was raw and overflowing with pain as he walked the half mile to the Sun Yat-Sen Memorial. He looked up and saw a pair of butterflies in a mating dance flying overhead.

Now I feel contempt for you like Beethoven does. You little insignificant insects keep showing us humans what we do not have, whether it is a straw or a lover!

Tears were raining down Chaing's face when he approached Beethoven, nursing a glass of wine at the bar.

"You tasted bitterness," Beethoven said as he took out one of his notebooks.

Chaing took his pen from his pocket and wrote. *She is spoken for. She insulted you, too.*

"Really? How so?" Beethoven asked.

She took your consummate score and threw it in the recycling.

"But I almost did the same when I was rejected. I almost burned some drafts of my scores when I went through a depression, I am glad I didn't, as they included an outline for my *Fifth Symphony*," Beethoven said.

She had more concern for the butterflies than me. Chaing pressed his pen so hard that the barrel nearly snapped. Beethoven leaned back, folded his hands in his lap, and allowed Chaing to continue venting.

"The butterflies were the first thing I noticed when I came here. They are symbols of resurrection, are they not? Look at me, I can do nothing that is worthwhile now. I am still the person I was when I was alive: a composer yes, but still deaf, and still an alcoholic. Only now no one will remember my work other than when the garbage truck drives by," Beethoven said.

Can't you look at it as honoring it? Chaing wrote then gestured emphatically with upturned palms. *Your work is so beautiful that it motivates people to do the right thing by the earth, to not abuse it. Your music moves the hearts of even the most stoic of people.*

Beethoven squinted his eyes, furrowed his brow, and began to bite his lower lip as if pained by Chaing's suggestion.

"Young man, you still have your whole life ahead of you. I just have my legacy and to be marooned here constantly with garbage trucks playing my score is hardly ideal. Why, I am starting to consider my deafness to be a blessing in death."

The two men sat, and soon the unmistakable sounds of the recorded music could be heard. As the truck approached, the glasses vibrated, visible even to a deaf man. When the trucks neared, Beethoven got up abruptly, gathering his wine bottle and scores, and hurried to the street. When the trucks stopped, Beethoven did not even wait for the trash collector to dismount. Angrily, the composer tossed the empty wine bottle against the recycling compactor. It shattered into a thousand pieces before being consumed. He then crumpled his scores into his hands, and with a look of malice on his face, deposited them in the garbage truck.

Chaing, who had followed the composer out into the street, turned a ghastly white. "You just threw your whole legacy in the trash!" Chaing said, forgetting that his friend could not hear him.

"I am not going to wallow in self-pity, either, at least in terms of my music. I am going to accept that my career ended when I died."

Chaing followed Beethoven back inside, shouting, yet knowing Beethoven could not hear him. "You have done no better than the girl I just asked to marry me!"

Beethoven sighed and beckoned the waiter for another drink, a pair of butterflies landed on the table in between the two men.

"They must be tired."

"Living one's dreams, whether one succeeds in them or not, is tiring," Beethoven said as if he had heard Chaing's words. As the waiter placed down a fresh glass of wine in front of him Beethoven continued. "When I was alive all, I could think of was producing music. Never did I think it would be reproduced to the degree it is now in the twenty-first century."

"Then your ego should be satisfied. Theoretically, I should be the one who is upset over my fresh loss. I can also see that you have selective hearing," Chaing said.

"We are all human," Beethoven slammed his fist on the table sending the two mating butterflies into the air. "But I respect the fact that my feelings do not make sense to you," the composer said. He took a sip of wine.

Chaing glanced at the butterflies whose gauzy silhouettes he could still make out. He watched as the male chased the female undeterred Chaing smiled, knowing finally that he would not continue to wallow in self-pity, as did the great composer, tending to his wine like an open wound which had just had salt rubbed in it.

Octaves of Love

The Manneken Pis

I can feel the red satin jacket slipping off my shoulders and the white powdered wig coming off the crown of my head. I feel like Christ when he was undressed, when he was taken down from the cross.

For five hundred years, I—a statue of a little boy—have supplied drinking water to all of Brussels from my loins. Once I was a legend, but now they dress me in bombastic costumes and change them every month. People passed by and took pictures of me when I was clothed like Mozart this past May, and a doctor last June. The gargoyles adorning the Hôtel de Ville, the opulent town hall behind me, laugh. As they see me in my full glory, they mock me. I wonder how I will be dressed this month.

Wait, wait—I see a black coat. It looks like something a groom might wear to a wedding, or possibly something a man might wear to a funeral. The costume changer puts it on me. It feels snug, but I don't see any pants this time. Now they are putting something in my hands. It is quite heavy. It must weigh several kilograms or so. It is golden in color.

Wait, is it a saxophone?

Yes, it is and how apropos, as it is the anniversary of the inventor's birthday, Adolph Sax.

Look at me, a buffoon! At least when I was Mozart, some busty blonds and slender brunettes came to admire me. Now, what can I expect to attract? For you see, all I have ever wanted is a relationship with a beautiful woman. Perhaps all is not lost. If I play the instrument that has been given me, if I play this saxophone, women will throw themselves at me.

The Alto Saxophone

I can't say the view is great to see a childish boy brashly urinating in public. I wonder why they do not turn him off. The city has modern plumbing. He is squeezing me too tight on my keys, and his lips around my reed are suffocating. No wonder I sound like an animal in a slaughterhouse. People are turning away, actually fleeing from the statue. Normally, he is a great tourist attraction as synonymous with Brussels as Trafalgar Square's Lions are with London, or the Trevi fountain is to Rome. Wait. Look down, someone dropped a cap at the Manneken's feet and is putting money in it.

"I'll give you twenty Euros to stop playing!" the man yells. But the statue is determined and only plays me louder. When he stops to catch his breath, I manage to get a word in.

"Why are you so hell bent on playing me?" I ask the statue. "You will get more positive attention if you just hold me."

"I don't want the attention to be on you. Everyone knows why the mayor and the town council have donned me with this outfit for the month," the statue says angrily. "Besides I have an ulterior motive."

"Really? And what is that?" I ask before the Manneken attempts to play me again, producing another ear-piercing shriek, a sound that only children make when they first start to learn.

"I want to attract a woman. It is well known that your sultry sounds which are played in jazz bars will attract them."

"Well, you are only scaring them away," I tell him.

Now a woman approaches. She looks all of nineteen. Her long blonde hair comes down to her waist. She has radiant blue eyes and a triangular nose. Upon seeing her, the Manneken grasps me harder. It is as if he is trying to control himself, or me, all the more. Now he blows softly, but it is too soft, and no sound emanates forth. He then overcompensates and plays what sounds like someone flatulating.

"How rude," the woman says, turning away, but not before dropping one euro into the hat. "I, too, will give you money if you only cease playing."

As the day goes on some tourists take videos of the escapade with their phones but none show an interest in the Manneken. When night falls and the statue boy is exhausted, I try to reason with him.

"You are now more a celebrity than you were when the day began. Why, I wouldn't be surprised if you are the top video on *YouTube*, *Tik Tok*, and all the other social media websites. Who knows? Maybe if you stop playing for the rest of the month and if you are given a better costume, like perhaps that of Elvis, which I know is in the museum that houses your outfits, you might attract a woman.

"I can't wait. It is summer. I have needs," The Manneken replies.

"Well, please leave me out of them. I understand that we are bound at the arms literally for the next thirty days, but I really do not want to be part of this. I think more highly of women than you."

"Is that so?" The Manneken shoots back.

"Why yes, it is," I say.

"Prove it," the Manneken challenges.

"How can I when I am stuck to you? Look, if you want a wife or a relationship, let me go to Paris, The City of Lights, the capital of romance, and I'll woo the perfect bride for you."

"Fine," the Manneken says. "I accept the offer."

The statue proceeds to unhook me from the lanyard that has been hung around his neck.

"Give me a week," I say. "But remember I can woo the woman you desire, but I can't teach you how to treat her."

"Just worry about the task at hand," the statue calls after me as I make my way to the train station, exhausted and full of spittle from a most uncouth boy.

***

The ride to Paris is uneventful. The train takes a circuitous route and swings through Antwerp, the diamond capital of the world, before heading west to Paris. I practice a few scales in my sleeping car and clean my reed, which has been chipped. I can feel that I have lost my zest. I feel so contaminated from the lips of that wretched boy.

The train pulls into Paris the next morning, and my first stop is to a music store where I replace my reed. I take a walk along the Avenue des Champs-Élysées, playing as I go. Heads start to turn, even the Parisian artists, who are constantly adjusting their berets as the wind blows so they can still see what they are painting, look up from their work. Children stop frolicking in the fountains to stare. Even the prostitutes, who are sulking in the alleyways, peer around the corners to glance at me. I want to be close to the center of town, to the tourists and culture of the city, so I find a small, cozy loft to rent on the left bank of the Seine overlooking the world-famous art museum, the Louvre. I watch the sun set, and then, as the first stars come out, the Eiffel Tower is illuminated.

A light breeze is blowing. My crooning sounds, which slowly grow louder and louder, can be heard on the wide thoroughfares that Paris is famous for. I play up and down, my whole range letting the valves do the work, knowing that my music will attract candidates for The Manneken.

The Venus De Milo

I am used to being admired. Tourists, archaeologists, and scientists alike have gazed at me for nearly two thousand years. In the hallowed institution of the Louvre, where it is so packed with locals and tourists that security is often unable to stop people touching me, I have had my fair share of unwanted advances. Tourists have fondled my breasts and kissed my navel, all while I gaze out silently across the hall. It could be worse. I doubt that most of the tourists have noble intentions, but some are able to overlook my deformity. There are those who are respectful, those who keep a five-foot distance and gaze at my beauty and contemplate it. It is for these people that I wish I had arms. Oh, how I would love to embrace them, to thank them for seeing me with the reverence that the curators do.

On this hot July night, the Louvre closes up as it always does. After the public leaves, the *Anubis* statue from the Egyptian section gives a yowling yawn, stretches out and goes to sleep. His loud snoring can be heard in the cavernous hallways of the Sully Wing. Leonardo's *Mona Lisa* unfolds her hands and rubs her cheeks wearily, as she has been gazed at more than any other artwork here and is tired of it. *Lady Liberty Leading the People* by Delacroix waves the tricolor French flag urging the revolutionaries onward.

If the public stayed here at night, they would be spellbound by what goes on, but to me this is all old hat. I'm bored. I am just about to doze off to sleep when I hear through a window, carelessly left open by security, the sensual sounds of a saxophone.

***

As I enter the loft, he doesn't look up but keeps playing, his muscular neck pulsating as the air rises through his valves. His keys move up and down rhythmically, like the tongue of an experienced kisser dancing with that of his lover's on the Pont Alexandre III Bridge on a snowy New Year's Eve with The Eiffel Tower in the background. The air comes out of his bell with such an intensity that, were he not alone, one could think he was making love to a woman.

Perhaps to me.

The Alto Saxophone

Her smoothness is legendary, the winds of time have not eroded her eternal youth, and all her curves are flawless. The crevices and cracks that were left by time are positioned so perfectly that even I, a musical instrument, can hold them as if they were carved just for me. We move across the bed in sync, the squeaky springs of the mattress move up and down with us. It is as if we have been making love for decades and we know every inch of each other, but all is new at the same time. After climaxing I fall asleep in her arms, my reed in her mouth. I feel her warm breath slowing down, her hands letting up pressure on my keys signaling that The Venus has been satisfied.

I am glowing. I am drunk on love as I descend the stairs of my home at the Louvre. I cannot wait for the museum to shut again so I can return to my lover. I pass the coat check, which I never looked at before, and then make my way to the ticket booth. I am about to continue to the Sully Wing where my perch is located when I notice the writing above the kiosk with script on one side and numbers on the other.

My happiness disappears, as I look at how much it costs an adult—ten euros—to enter the museum; a child pays five; a senior citizen pays seven; disabled people are free. Tears replace my smile as I read.

Am I nothing more than a prostitute that people pay to come and see? Does the world only see me as a whore? My heart races in anger and sadness.

I pass the *Anubis* and the *Mona Lisa* as I continue to my gallery. They are still sleeping. I am tempted to wake them, to tell them about the reprehensive truth of what I have just learned, but I restrain myself, avoiding the questions they will surely have about where I was last night.

Through the day, I try to hold my head up high. I try to reframe things. When a Japanese couple walk up to me, I try to imagine how much they must have spent on airfare to make my acquaintance. I am starting to feel a little better, but these thoughts are interrupted when a man in a wheelchair, attended by a burly man who is clearly impatient and annoyed, stand in front of me.

"This is the beautiful piece of art I have come here to see," the man in the wheelchair says. "Then I promise you we can leave, and I will pay you your full day's wages."

"You had best include the admission fee I had to pay," the burly man says, then he mumbles to himself. "Who would want to pay to see this disfigured woman anyway?'

I try to hold my position with dignity, but it is harder than ever now that I know the reality of my existence.

Thankfully, I hear the bells of Notre Dame telling me that it is five o'clock and that The Louvre will close its doors soon. When the museum is finally emptied of its visitors, in the dark quiet, I hear the melodious notes of the saxophone floating in through the window, and I begin to sprout arms.

The Alto Saxophone

When I awake the next morning, I am in a stupor. I rub the sleep from my eyes, make some coffee, and wait for the lovely Venus to wake up. I look at the sunrise while sitting at the small table across from the bed. I must admit she is not the female I had thought I would attract.

I am looking at The Venus affectionately and contemplating how I will have trouble giving her up to the Manneken as I am smitten by her. I am going over this dilemma in my head when I notice something out of the corner of my eye. The Venus, who had her hands crossed under the pillow, like a dog might when it rests its head on its paws when it sleeps, has turned over and to my surprise, I see that her arms are retracting, shriveling like sausages when they are placed over an open flame. Within thirty seconds they are the renowned stumps that can be seen in every postcard and every photo that has ever been taken of her. I watch in her half sleep as she turns again and tries to embrace me, but all she grasps is air. I cannot help but to be moved.

Venus De Milo

"I have never been played like that before," he tells me "I felt like I was in the hands of Charlie Parker or Dexter Gordon.

"And I have never had coffee made for me," I reply. "I have always been photographed and gawked at. When I awoke, I expected to find a five euro note on the bed stand, and for you to be gone with your sights set on someone else."

"How could that be possible?" the saxophone beams. "Come, let us go for a stroll along the river and continue to enjoy each other's company."

It is Sunday as we walk by the Seine and the city is quiet. There is not a soul on the street.

"Have you ever left the museum before?" the saxophone inquires.

"No, I had no reason to. Nothing gave me the desire. I assumed that all admirers of mine were there for my beauty, but no one ever saw the full-formed me until you. Besides, how can you really tell what a man is thinking when he is behind a camera?"

We reach the Jardin du Luxembourg and stop to look at some of the statues of famous French citizens and feel envious that there is no cost to see them. My partner looks at a male nude of a French writer. My lover's face contours as if in pain.

"What's wrong?" I ask the saxophone.

Hesitantly, he answers me "A friend asked me to do him a favor."

"What type of favor?" I ask.

The saxophone leans forward and kisses me on the cheek. "I'll tell you later," he whispers in my ear before we disappear into a sea of fog. While we walk, he asks me to go to Brussels with him. He tells me that he would like to show me where he is from and for me to meet his friends. I hope that our relationship has the chance to grow by octaves and this means that he intends for me to be part of his life, but I am also just as aware and fearfully entertain the possibility that the saxophone may change his mind about me, that his infatuation may evaporate when we leave Paris.

The Alto Saxophone

As soon as the train has cleared the end of the platform so The Venus cannot disembark until we get to Brussels, I confess.

"My trip to Paris was supposed to be nothing more than a sojourn with a very specific purpose. I had not expected to meet you," I begin in a somber voice.

"Love does work in mysterious ways. I never intended to leave The Louvre before," The Venus says.

"No, no you don't understand," I say anxiously. The air goes through my reed in bursts making my voice shake. "I was sent here by my captor, The Manneken Pis. He gave me instructions to find a suitable bride for him, and that task is proving harder than I thought, as I did not expect to find someone with whom I myself have feelings for."

"Why do you have to follow instructions?" The Venus asks as tears spring to her eyes. My heart begins to crack at the sight of her pain. "We were hardly traditional when we met, being intimate on our first meeting and falling in love."

"Let me see how I can explain this in a way that might possibly make any sense to you," I say, as I take a deep breath. "Like you, I am usually a museum piece. I was only taken out of my case so that I could be the custom prop for The Manneken Pis as it is the anniversary of the birth of my inventor, Adolph Sax. He only let me go to Paris on the condition that I brought him back a bride. I fear that if I do not comply, I will be behind glass forever to be seen by a few jazz aficionados who come to the house of Adolph Sax. From what you have told me your experience as a museum exhibit was fairly pleasant until very recently, but for me it never was. Now, the thought of giving you to another man is unbearable. But I know things will work in our favor. Please believe me."

The Venus takes a few minutes to process my thoughts. I wouldn't be surprised if she feels that I am prostituting her out using her to buy my freedom. She probably thinks of me like the clerk in the Louvre that handles the admission fees.

"I understand, I understand," The Venus says softly as we cross into Belgium. "You must feel like Abraham when he was told to sacrifice his son. I will be your Isaac," The Venus nuzzles my reed.

Fifteen minutes before sunset, we arrive at the main square, The Venus right beside me, where The Manneken is waiting.

"I have kept my word," I begin. "Monsieur Pis, may I present to you Mademoiselle De Milo."

The Venus De Milo

As the saxophone steps away, I am aghast at what I see. There is a roguishly devilish little boy in black suit with his genitalia in hand. I would have thought that he might have gone to some effort, perhaps even a facial expression of embarrassment, that would say he wishes he could stop exposing himself to me and urinating. But no, he just smiles and continues to look out over the square as if he is God's gift to humanity.

"This is the creature you brought me?" I hear the Manneken say in disgust. "How can I be even remotely attracted to her? She has no arms!"

I am greatly relieved when The Manneken rejects me. This must be what my beloved saxophone knew what would happen, and as the sun goes down and darkness envelops the square, my messianic arms begin to return. I embrace my saxophone and I start to play.

But to my horror, The Manneken says. "Forgive me, I was mistaken," He adjusts his collar and for the moment stops urinating. "I was not my best, as you can see, and perhaps my insecurity got in the way. I now see your beauty and if you are so inclined I would like to have a dance with you."

My hope and happiness vanishes when I turn to see that a crowd has come out of their flats and pubs to listen. They begin to lay money beside me, now paying to hear my music rather than only look at my body. I am no longer a whore. The people gathered around me remain enraptured by our duet until the early hours of the morning. The Manneken can no longer control his rage. He lets forth the urine that he has been holding, so that it splashes my lover and me.

"The only reason you can attract people is due to your playing. When you lose your arms again," The Manneken bellows. "You will be nothing!"

"You are wrong sir, wrong," the Alto Saxophone calls out, "I will always be with her with limbs or none."

"Get out of my sight you traitorous brass idiot!" The Manneken shouts out.

I am free at last and safe with my lover even as my arms disappear with the rising of the sun.

***

The Manneken Pis

I try to brush off last night's events. The Venus, she was not worth my time. Nor was that stupid saxophone. I am looking forward to my next costume change. Perhaps it will be one without such a pathetic prop. I spend the rest of the month looking forward to the first of August, as it will be peak tourist time and perhaps then I will find the mate worthy of my beauty, the pride of all Brussels.

Finally, the first of the month arrives. I stand proudly as my suit is removed and dozens of tourists film and photograph the ceremony. It is an overcast day and the flashes from their cameras are quite blinding so I cannot get a very good look at any prospective partners. I breathe a sigh of relief as my new jacket comes on. It is made of satin and is much softer than my previous outfit. I smile when I spot an attractive ginger-haired woman who is photographing me. I contemplate what to say to her and even considering stopping my urinating when I feel the new prop balanced next to me.

"I wonder why they are giving him a mock rifle." The woman's girlfriend laughs as she snaps several photographs.

The ginger haired woman joins in her laughter, holding her camera to her face, "He is nothing but a silly boy who can't control his bodily functions."

The women are foolishly mistaken. Clearly, they are unable to see my manliness. Afterall, I single-handedly provided water for this city for hundreds of years. Have they all forgotten my value?

Would they realize how simple and shallow they are if they had to pay for the privilege of gazing upon me and taking my photograph?

The Hungarian Salami

Budapest, my Budapest. How do I love thee?

Your nearly two dozen districts straddle the mighty Danube, having withstood domination by the Turks and the Austrians. Now Hungarians luxuriate in the baths that had been corrupted by occupiers, cleansing themselves of Asiatic influences as they play chess on floating chessboards and plot the next move. In time, the lands of Romania, Slovakia, and Ukraine will be restored. Our new empire will be larger than that of the former House of Hapsburg.

If only this renaissance, this rebirth of Magyar greatness, would flower even faster. One can walk down the street to my place of residence on Mihályi Táncsics Street near the Erdődy Palace, where the Bartók Museum is across the road from the synagogue. Here you will find bastards of our great culture in the guises of shifty Slovaks, thieving gypsies, resentful Romanians, and wandering Jews. They are not here for the music of the great Bartók; they are lining up outside Katz's Deli, my place of residence.

My home:

A trinity of dilapidated stools, whose tops are secured with rusting screws, face the window that looks out to the cobblestoned street. Below me, behind the stools and the narrow floor space, are two glass cases. One is for the kosher meats and one of the others—pork products prosciutto, Spanish chorizo, and Corsican ham. This miasma of heterogeneity flies in the face of our Zeitgeist.

Hungary for Hungarians!

Inside, the space is so narrow that customers must stand shoulder-to-shoulder as they wait to call out their purchases, their money clutched in their greedy hands. The heavy golden cash register is manned by the Jew. Behind him on a small table a vintage gramophone plays degenerate klezmer music and deviant Yiddish folksongs.

So here I am Nimrod, an air-dried salami, hanging in agony.

My only joy arrives at noon when the youth of the Arrow Cross Party parade past the deli as they have been, like clockwork, for the past few weeks. Hanging from my perch and through the store front window, I watch the boys in their brown shirts, with flags of our ancestral land knitted on their shoulders, playing drums and singing Hungarian folk songs.

Hungary for Hungarians.

Each Friday afternoon, a new order of foreign meats is delivered. The Jew unpacks the boxes and arranges the wares in the display case below me. He hurries to finish before the sun goes down and his Sabbath begins. He then locks the door and hurries off.

Foolish man.

As soon as he is gone, without fail, the new arrivals begin to babble anxiously in fear. And with good reason, for unlike me, who is perfectly air dried and will last forever, they will, if not sold soon, simply expire.

Moving from west to east geographically they converse in their Romantic tongues, Spanish, French, Italian, and Romanian, all of which are mawkish to the ear. First the Spanish chorizo speaks, followed by the Corsican ham, followed by the Italian prosciutto, and finally the Romanian pastrami.

"Tengo miedo no tenemos mucho tiempo," the Spanish chorizo begins.

"Si je ne suis pas consumé ma vie aura été vaine," the Corsican ham says.

"Essere venduti e nostra salvezza," the Parma Ham comments.

"Starea asta în care ne aflăm este atât de străină," the Romanian pastrami laments.

Their language is nothing but queer, incomprehensible, and offensive babble, an insult to me—an insult to my country. I have no choice but to endure the chatter of these heretics until finally I drift into a restless slumber.

I dream.

***

I dream of the Great Babylonian King Nimrod, my namesake.

On the vast floodplain I see his army of workers, stripped half-naked to their waists, with loops of crude leather tethered to their shoulders. They haul massive stones up earthen ramps, sweat careening off their brows like the cataract waterfalls of the mighty Danube. What is the work they are doing? They are building the Tower of Babel, reaching to the heavens to challenge God himself.

"Onward," King Nimrod commands. He pounds his bronze staff into the hard, arid ground. "If we have truly been made in the image of God, surely he will let us gaze upon his face."

I dream.

I dream of countless nights and days as the laborers toil, in complete unison, at their task. During the arduous ordeal many die of exertion. But their sacrifice for the greater good, our return to the Garden of Eden, and it does not go unrewarded. They are lionized in lofty eulogies by King Nimrod himself.

"We are courting greatness," King Nimrod proclaims. "The Almighty will have to draw us back into his bosom."

The men build higher and higher, farther and farther from the ground. The laborers are more and more exhausted, and they begin to question.

"Why does The Almighty not embrace us?" the workers cry out. "When will we gaze at the feet of God?"

I listen.

I listen to the voices rising as one; they speak in a single tongue, one language, one dialect. However, as the weeks drag on, more of the workers fall to their deaths. Soon the supplicative entreaties become belligerent and revolutionary.

"If God will not present Himself to us, we will present ourselves to Him," they shout. "We will show Him that we are as worthy of respect and recognition as He is. After all, who would He be without us to worship Him? He is nothing!"

And so still higher they build, until the ground is no longer visible from their summit. It is obscured by the clouds that drift across the sky like mercurial messengers.

After a decade of building King Nimrod proclaims, "Should we not gaze upon God's face by the end of the week, it will be evident that He does not value us, and I will be forced to take His place."

Not moments after the King announced his intent, the ramp upon which the workers stand begins to twist and tremble and shake. Many of the workers are thrown from the scaffolding, falling to their death. Those that survive begin to beg. They beseech the very One they were chastising. "Forgive us," they cry. "Save us."

I watch.

I watch as the workers stop laying bricks. One by one, they abandon their work and flee. It would seem that fear has supplanted any former desire to challenge God. They think now only of how to survive. They scream out in new languages that I do not understand, many languages, a jumble of sounds. I watch King Nimrod, left alone, forsaken, defeated, and humiliated.

In my dream all becomes clear: the descendants of Nimrod's sons, Hunor and Magor, the ancestors of Hungary, must be restored to their former glory. Greater Hungary must be unified, and King Nimrod's death avenged.

I am awake.

I know what I must do.

***

That Saturday morning when the shop is closed and empty—the Jew is taking his day of rest—I take comfort in my unobstructed view of the street. As the sun breaks and the church bells ring, I am pleasantly surprised by an early morning parade by the Arrow Cross Party youth. I watch them pass.

I expect them to be carrying their drums and flags, but instead, see them carry a bucket and paint rollers. They stop in front of my home. They put down their bucket and face the window. One of the boys climbs a ladder they have bought, while the others steady it. Another boy soaks a roller in white paint, and hand to hand, they pass it along, and the boy on the ladder commences. He is concentrating on a single straight line, which then makes a sharp turn at a right angle. He starts again, and then again, and when the lines come together, they create a magnificent swastika. The Hitlerite symbol is large and occupies the center of the deli's storefront window.

Underneath the swastika—even in reverse—I can clearly make out the words.

Hungary for Hungarians! All others out.

"Heil Hitler! Long live Horthy," the boys yell in unison, in one beautiful Hungarian voice, before moving on with their bucket to the next place of Jewish commerce. Oh, how I wish I could follow them and watch as the swastika replicates along the streets. However, my fellow deli residents do not appear to feel the same.

The chorizo cries out, "En la España fascista no es diferente."

Then I hear the Corsican. "Une nation ne se définit pas uniquement par une langue."

"Il mundo e diventato piu piccolo la mescolanza culturale e inevitabile," the Parma ham adds.

Must I listen to this gibberish? I don't see the Frenchmen making efforts to speak English. Nor the Spaniard. Nor the Romanian. Why should we Hungarians be expected to behave differently?

But it is the comment by the pastrami that really angers me, I only heard half of it. I'm not certain what it is saying, but it seems that this one is claiming Hungary was better when ruled by the Hapsburgs with those Czechs, Slovenes, Croats, Serbs, Slovaks, Poles, Austrians, Bosnians, and those Ukrainians all mixed together.

He is most grossly mistaken.

And one day I will get my chance to prove it.

***

Sundays are usually slower days. Few of my compatriots come to the deli, as they are rightfully in church. On these days, the Jew usually follows the same routine. He kisses his ridiculous mezuzah, unlocks the shop, immediately starts up his ancient gramophone.

Today, however, is different. When Moshe rounds the corner and sees the "artwork" in his shop, he becomes perfectly still. I watch as his body stiffens. I can see the ligaments in his hands contracting. He winces as if in pain. He is so close to the glass that his breath takes shape like fog rising off the Danube.

His hands shaking, he fumbles for his keys and unlocks the shop. He forgets to pay homage to his God, forgets to kiss the mezuzah. He does not, as is customary, entertain his soul with his klezmer music. Instead, the Jew quickly fills a bucket with warm water, grabs a sponge, and rushes back outside. I watch him in his futile task, until he gives up, and comes back to attend to the counter.

When the church bells ring at noon I spot a woman dressed in rags, carrying an infant bundled in her arms. She has copper bangles around her wrists and cloth wrapped around her head. I recognize her as someone who often frequents the deli on Sundays, surely a gypsy.

When the Jew sees her, he waves almost frantically, inviting her in. I watch as the woman approaches the door, yet when she sees the shadow in the glass, the ghost of a swastika, she draws her baby close, turns, and walks swiftly back in the direction from which she came.

I watch as the Jew refills his pail, hurries outside, and once again sets to work trying to remove the paint from his storefront. Every so often he looks down from his ladder to see if any customers have come, but much to my happiness, none do. My pleasure is heightened when, half an hour later, a boy from the Arrow Cross band comes to the door of the deli.

"Good afternoon," the Jew says. Soapy water from his sponge drips to the ground. He climbs down from his ladder. "How may I help you?"

"You can close down your shop, you stiff-necked Jew," the boy says. He spits on the glass case where the new arrivals lay. "Look at the Spanish, the Italians, and French. Look at the Romanians. There is nothing Hungarian here." Then the boy looks up. "That!" he cries. "That air dried paprika infused salami. That is your redemption."

***

By the time Wednesday rolls around, the Jew has cut his prices. Now symphonies from Bartók and concertos from Lizt boom forth from his gramophone. A Hungarian flag also flies outside the pole screwed into the wall where the mezuzah used to be.

How pathetic!

Still no customers come.

The ham, the pastrami, the various displaced cheeses begin to expire.

As he must, the Jew disposes the unsold foreigners into the trash behind the store. Never in my history of hanging above the counter have I heard so many rats scurry toward the deli. I hear them gorge themselves on The Spaniard, The Frenchman, The Italian, and The Romanian, before scurrying off to the sewers.

A bell jangles above the door and the boy walks inside. "I see that you have changed your inventory," he says.

"Yes," The Jew lowers his eyes. "I have. All I have left is this salami from the Bekes," he says. "I hear it goes very well with the local wine."

The boy lifts his chin toward me. "I will take it."

The Jew unhooks me from the hook that hangs from the ceiling. As I am lowered onto the scale, I see that my time has come. My destiny has arrived.

Where King Nimrod failed, I, his namesake, will succeed.

The boy tucks me under his arm, and I am free!

Outside for the first time, I will see the capital of my great nation in all its glory. It is evening, and the streets are quiet. The boy carries me past parliament, past the world-famous Baths of Budapest, and past the Hungarian State Opera House.

The Vizslas, the Hungarian hunting dogs, are walking off their leashes. They are proud and unafraid. Captives no more!

We pass St Mátyás church. I see a long line of people waiting to enter through the massive cathedral doors, heading to evening Mass. I can hear the homilies spoken in Hungarian, not Latin.

Behold King Nimrod!

We pass St. Istávan's Basilica where the right hand of St. Istávan himself resides, preserved forever under glass. It beckons me as I embark on my crusade to rid Hungary of foreign tongues.

As we walk farther, the neighborhood begins to change. Here, the elegant cobblestones of Central Pest are overturned, some broken completely in half. They have not been repaired, it would seem, in years. The gutters which run alongside the streets are cracked and broken, many are clogged with detritus. Here? This is where the good strong workers of Budapest live, the lifeblood of the Hungarian nation? This is an outrage.

Behold Nimrod.

The boy carries me inside to his flat and lays me on his kitchen table. I am ready to meet the fate I have longed for, that I always knew, one day, would come.

The boy puts two pieces of rye bread on the plate; my humble coffin. He spreads a thick layer of mustard on each slice; frankincense and myrrh that only the holiest of people are graced with during burial. The serrated blade; a final blessing. He cuts into my flesh. The boy holds my body as if I were The Pieta and brings me closer to his mouth.

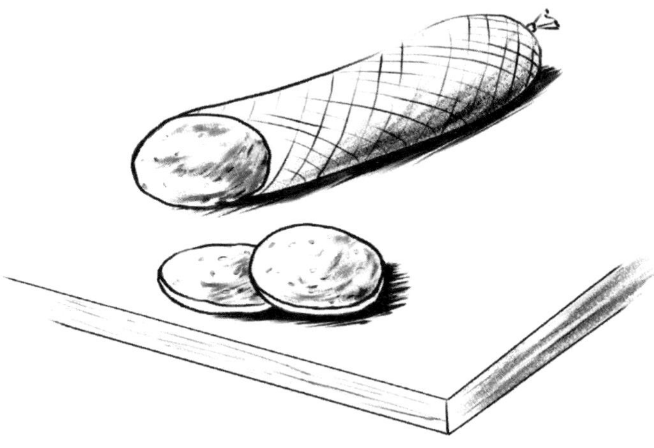

In mere moments, I will be consumed, but my sacrifice will have challenged the international order. I will have purged Hungary of its heterogeneity. Because of me, the Shifty Slovaks, Thieving gypsies, Resentful Romanians, and the Wandering Jews will all soon be banished. And when all you hear is the beautiful Hungarian language, you will know it is I who has rebuilt The Tower of Babel.

I dream. I watch. I am awake.

In a single bite, I am gone.

Mouth Vernon

That evening, with great apprehension the general (soon to be president), knew that the entire state of the union (or his assessment of it) rested on how well he would be able to deliver his speech, which in turn depended on how well his prosthetic worked. Washington felt the weight of the world in his mouth, or rather, of the foreign *teeth* in his mouth. His newly fabricated dentures consisted of the shaved down teeth of donkeys, horses, and cows, as well as those composed of ivory from hippopotamuses and elephants, not to mention one incisor, one bicuspid, and one molar that were courtesy of his slave, Thomas. With Thomas standing by his side, the general thought of the upcoming tobacco harvest. This year there had been a bumper crop, one with which he was hoping to pay off the debt he had gone into, all to finance his dentures.

"My fel- fell-fellow Am-am-mericans," Washington practiced, stumbling over the first line of his speech while looking at his new set of teeth. He stood in front of a full-length mirror while Thomas, in the reflection behind him, powdered the general's wig.

"T-T-T-oday," Washington continued. "Today, we are gathered here for a historic occasion." He took a deep breath, pleased that he had managed to get through a sentence without any impediments. Washington inhaled as Thomas gave the wig a last quaff, causing a week's worth of dust to erupt along with the mites that had made their home in it. Washington sneezed, the force of which caused his dentures to become unhinged and hang precariously from his sole natural, albeit dead, tooth.

"Blasted contraption," Washington bellowed. He opened his palm, landing it directly across Thomas' mouth. Thomas winced in pain, his mouth agape, exposing the holes that were a result of selling Washington his teeth on April 27th, 1789, for which he received three pounds and two shillings. He didn't utter a sound.

"I suppose I will have to do the howling in pain for both of us?" Washington said, after he had managed to put his dentures back in place. "Well, don't just stand there," he berated Thomas. "Put my wig on so that I may practice again. Then leave me be. Perhaps I will be more successful if I am alone."

Thomas grasped the edges of the wig with both hands and gingerly reached over his master's crown before depositing it, then made himself scarce. Thomas descended the stairs, out into the yard of the main plantation house, and made his way to the barn where he slept. Thomas crossed a mile of tobacco field, using the full moon and the lights of the fireflies that hovered in the thick muggy air to guide him. As he crossed the stream that ran through the middle of the property, Thomas could hear the braying of donkeys and mooing of cattle. They too, without anesthetic, recently had their teeth extracted to create Washington's dentures. For two days Thomas tried in vain to feed the animals, but they refused to eat. Their gums, swollen and infected, bled to the touch from even the softest hay.

***

For two days, Washington continued to struggle with his dentures. Halfway through the speech he found that his mouth was too dry, and that in spite of frequent drinks of water he was unceasingly parched. After an hour of rehearsing, Washington gave up. He glanced at the pocket watch hanging from its chain. It was midnight, and he would need to be on the road at dawn. The general undressed and got into his night clothes, removing his dentures and placing them on the table beside him, then snuffed out his bedside candle. The general fell asleep, his mouth wide open, his lone dead tooth standing like a sentry watching the moon as it made its way across the night sky.

***

While Washington slept fitfully, one of Thomas' incisors struggled to shift itself slightly so as to be comfortable, wedged in between the elephant ivory and hippopotamus's canine. "What's in this for us?" the tooth asked.

"Nothing, brother, nothing," Thomas' bicuspid answered.

"That is why I intend to make Washington as uncomfortable as possible," Thomas' molar said. "The trauma he inflicted upon us when he pulled us out from our native mouth has to be repaid. I am not about to be a Mouth Vernon for his venomous oration."

***

By the time Washington was dressed and ready to begin the five-day journey to New York, Thomas had already been up for hours. He had fed and watered the horses and saddled them. He had polished his master's carriage and loaded it with provisions: salted pork, gourmandise cheese, an abundance of corn, and plenty of ale. He had also packed the master's traveling desk, an inkwell, ink, and Washington's wig. Before Washington climbed the steps, he turned around one last time, shielded his face from the sun, and gazed out over his fields of tobacco.

"I want to make it back in time so I can oversee the harvest," Washington said, sitting beside his wig, which lay on the satin seat of the carriage.

Stopping at an inn the first night, Washington cursed, trying to numb his pain with ale as the springs of his dentures dug into his gums. Outside, Thomas ate and cried softly to himself as he bit into the corn, the soft tissues inside his mouth not accustomed to eating.

They drove through Virginia and Maryland. They arrived in Philadelphia and stopped for the night, where Washington was greeted with great fanfare. Despite the rocky terrain, Washington spent most of the time editing his speech. When they reached Jersey City, the pair boarded a ferry and crossed the Hudson, disembarking at a pier not far from Wall Street. Thomas guided his master's carriage downtown to Federal Hall where Washington was to be the first inaugurated president of the newly formed United States of America.

With Thomas at his side holding his speech, Washington ascended the dais. Those assembled, an overwhelming majority of men, waited to hear the General speak. The crowd included those of every trade, from coopers to merchants, sailors to goldsmiths, printers to attorneys. All in attendance were white, save the few dozen free people of color who had come to hear the speech as well.

When the cheering had died down, Washington took three deep breaths and began to speak. "My fellow Americans, we come together this day having ousted the British from our land."

He winced as he struggled to annunciate without the wire from his dentures digging into the back of his throat. No one seemed to notice, and the crowd erupted into cheer; the teeth listened.

"We have thrown off the yoke of colonialism and are here with God's help to establish a bicameral congress where all will have representation."

***

"Three fifths. He forgot to mention the three fifths," the bicuspid hissed. "That's how they are going to count us colored folk as three fifths of a person. They count animals as full beings. They count cattle by the head, but we are just three fifths. I'm so disgusted. I just want to jump ship now."

"Patience," the incisor counseled. "We need to wait until he lays out more of his vision. The more we hear, the more points we can potentially counter."

"I don't know. I don't know," the bicuspid said. "The longer we let Washington's tongue have its way, the angrier I get. That tongue is nothing more than an empty fallow field, and we are like the slaves working a tobacco field, planting the seeds of wealth and profit off the skin of our backs."

"He will reap what he sows. Patience and wait for my signal," the incisor said.

***

"Our ports are now free," Washington continued. "Free of the British menace and open for trade and free flowing commerce. Let livestock flow from the great plantations of the south to New York and Boston. Let finished goods, the textiles being woven in the mill towns by our fine women and girls of Lowell, Massachusetts and Canton, Connecticut be shipped south to Baltimore, Charleston, and Mobile. Now the fruits of labor can spproutttt. . ."

Washington began to hack. Thomas took the liberty to slap his master on the back a few times.

"We are being cued by the master himself," the bicuspid said.

"Which master?" the molar asked, "Washington or Thomas?"

"Does it really matter?" the bicuspid shot back.

"Of course, it does," the incisor interjected. "But now is not the time for debate. As soon as Washington is at a good angle, I am unhitching the springs."

***

The blows to Washington's back were not taken kindly by the general. Once Washington had regained composure he furrowed his brow in anger, the lines resembling the trenches that he had the soldiers dig in the war for independence. Washington turned his back to the crowd and raised his hand to strike Thomas.

Just before the blow landed, the incisor gave the signal.

Once the springs were unhinged, the three teeth freed themselves from the dentures and jumped out of the general's mouth, flying into Thomas' with ease.

And Thomas began to speak.

"But this new nation of ours can and will do better. It can surpass the British parliamentary system and have representation for all. It will free those in bondage, both the slave who toils in the fields from dusk till dawn and the woman who slaves over the loom, her fingers worn and bleeding. We can pass legislation that guarantees the humane treatment of our beasts of burden, donkey, cattle, and horses alike. All these things we can, and will, accomplish."

As Thomas spoke, the land-owning gentry, the merchants, and even the freed people of color, whose livelihoods were all threatened by Thomas' revolutionary ideas, couldn't evacuate the square fast enough. The morality being put forth was too costly for them to even begin to contemplate.

***

Upon arriving home, the first thing Washington did, even before taking care of his bodily functions, was to lock his dentures in his heavy oak desk so they could never speak such hogwash again.

When the cock crowed the next morning, Thomas and the others gathered in front of the master's house waiting for his orders, but none came. The harvest would go to ruin this year, the profits from tobacco meant to cover the cost for his teeth, a wash. The speech had been a disaster, and Washington would be in pain forever.

Maggot Wagon

From the plains of Budapest to the steppe outside Moscow, and the valleys near Varna we dine. We dine on a banquet which feeds not only our bodies but our souls. As the wounded soldiers come back to our wagon, either draped over ponies or on make-shift stretchers carried by their comrades, we poke our heads out from behind the canvas and go to work. We eviscerate the dead flesh, separate the wheat from the chaff, as we preserve the living tissue.

We have taken the Hippocratic Oath to do no harm. To us, consuming the dead flesh is the propagation and the continuation of life. War may exist, but what makes it bearable is that everyone survives.

We larva tear through the necrotic flesh, neutralizing odors and consuming bad humors and pus. Over the course of our time with the Great Khan, we treated the majority of his best warriors.

Rarely do we receive even the smallest bit of gratitude when the warriors return to the battlefield—courtesy of us—but praise is not why we do our job.

After we have matured, we will grow wings. We will fly off over the battlefields. We have heard rumors of horrible things that we cannot even dream of but have no confirmation of this.

This is life. This is our life. This is God's work. Oh, how our duty was truly such delectable bliss. In the winter of 1258, we reach the sandy plains surrounding the great city of Baghdad. The human scouts have brought back reports of the fabled metropolis. They speak of the mosque's golden domes and of the great madrassas, centers of learning. They speak of mighty aqueducts and public gardens, which boast terraced waterfalls flowing gracefully into ponds filled with lily pads and honeysuckle.

***

As our wagon lies at rest around the bonfire, the Kahn speaks to his warriors on the day before battle. "This will be a quicker affair than our other campaigns," he says. "The Arabs are lazy city dwellers. They are untrained in the ways of combat and only train for war once a year. We shouldn't have that many wounded, but they will have thousands upon thousands.

***

The night before engaging The Caliph of Baghdad, the soldiers light fires and use their shields as spits as they roast mutton, beef, and goats. They feast. However, when the morning sun appears, our routine changes. Instead of being taken behind a hill, as we would normally, our wagon is hitched to the team of horses. We are pulled to the back of the army as it advances across the hot sandy alluvial plain on which Baghdad sits. There are no mountains, or valleys, no place of refuge for us to set up our medical tent as we wait for the wounded to arrive back from battle.

For the first time we have an unobstructed view of the fighting. This time we can watch the battle. We peek out from the burlap sacks that cover us to observe the Khan riding out to the middle of the desert to meet with the Caliph. We hope that our foe will surrender. The Kahn allows all those whom he has defeated to go about their lives provided they pay taxes to fill his coffers.

How noble is the Khan to give our enemies the opportunity to lay down their arms to avoid bloodshed.

Not only are we proud of the Khan, but we are proud of ourselves for being part of this mighty confederation that has spread across Asia.

These exalted thoughts are only interrupted by the rumblings in our stomachs. Many of us have not eaten since the last minor skirmish at Basra, and we are hungry. We are relieved when the Khan rides back to confer with his generals.

He has his men divide the flanks, clearing a path for the archers so that they may fire their first volley of arrows before the cavalry charges ahead. For the first time, from under the burlap sack, we watch as the arrows fly in an arch over the enemy's advancing column.

We watch as our soldiers fall onto the dusty plain. Some do not get up. Blood runs freely, from skin, the muscle, and the organs, that have been pierced by arrows, soaking the dry, arid ground in dark red.

Our soldiers flee. They return to camp, fighting to get close to our hospital wagon, pushing each other aside. They grab us in handfuls, as if we were war booty, like the gold they pilfered when we sacked Budapest, like the beautiful icons that mesmerized them in the churches of Varna.

"Help us!" the soldiers cry, as they desperately place us on their gashes and tears.

We scour the wounds for dead flesh with the hundreds of eyes that line our bodies. We look for infected, rotting tissue, but none is found. The areas to which we have been applied are fresh wounds. We are helpless swimming in a sea of blood as many of the cuts have yet to clot. Thousands of us are swept away and drowned.

We cry as we watch our friends lift their heads, trying one last time with their lancet teeth to find any dead tissues, but to no avail. We watch as they breathe their last. Never have we gazed upon such sacrifices. In the distance, we see the enemy die, and worse, we see our men dishonor them. Our soldiers kick the Arab corpses and spit on them.

The behavior is heartbreaking. We cannot help but recall the campaign in Tibet some half a century ago when a great Buddhist prisoner who had been taken from a Lamastary told us the story of Lord Buddha.

Lord Buddha grew up a prince confined to a castle. His father did not want him to know what the real world was like. However, one day he escaped and saw a sick man. When he was taken back to the palace, he was upset, and his father was even more determined that he should not venture out again. Lord Buddha did venture out again to satisfy his curiosity about the real world. When he went out a second time, he saw a dead body. This, too, saddened him. It was after this encounter that Lord Buddha discovered that Moksha or liberation of the soul could be found in this lifetime.

When we heard this, we laughed under our breath. What is this *death*? What is a *soul*? What is *rebirth?*

For as long as we had traveled with the Khan, no one ever died. Everyone returned to battle, and surely like us, the enemy had maggots to heal them as well.

When night falls, the rest of our surviving wounded return to our camp. Our men nurse their wounds and eat a meager repast as they look after their agonizing wounds and cry out in pain.

By nightfall, when the fires are lit and the men are resting, we stop our work. We hold counsel amongst ourselves. We discuss what we have observed over a few short hours. Our eyes have been opened in much the same ways Lord Buddha's were hundreds of years ago. We decide to confront the Kahn. We serve him an ultimatum: strike a truce with the Caliph and withdraw from the campaign, or we will no longer heal your warriors. The Khan is furious.

"Why do you blame me? I have simply taught you your true nature," the Kahn bellows. "You also feast on death. Your survival depends on the flesh I provide."

But we stand firm. The wailing of the Khan's men and the realization he must have—that he will lose half his army to infected wounds—persuade him to ride out the next morning under a white flag to meet with the Caliph.

"I've agreed to what you have asked me," the Khan tells us. "We will bury our dead, and the Caliph his. Then we will return to Bukhara."

We ride atop the shoulders, and necks, and bodies of our wounded soldiers, doing our work. Between mouthfuls of rotting, decomposing, putrid flesh, we watch as our soldiers toss the bodies of the dead into long, shallow troughs dug into the sand and soil.

Are they worth so much less in death than they had been in life?

Is this what the Buddha saw?

Is this our life?

In the distance, we see the Muslims burying their dead with dignity and respect. They dig generous six-foot deep graves, wrap their deceased in the finest linen from the stores in their city and place their heads so that they face east in the direction of their holy city Mecca.

What ignorant blinded fools we have been. We will never trust the Kahn again, nor do we anticipate that he will keep his promise to end the war. We conspire to have those amongst us with wings to fly to the doors of the Kahn's tent to listen, seeing if we can glean anything about his upcoming plans for his army and for us.

We hear the Kahn drinking in his tent with his generals, conferring in a drunken state.

"Now is the time. If we attack at night and set their tents ablaze, we have a chance to be victorious."

Those amongst us listening, confront the Khan again. We hover by his ear and remind him of the arrangement to end the war—to make peace.

"I have never been defeated before, and I am not about to be now," the Kahn bellows. He stands. "I will not be threatened by those who do not risk death on the battlefield. Who are nothing more than scavengers."

The Kahn grabs a torch from outside his tent and makes his way to our wagon. Without hesitation, he touches the fire to the burlap covering and it alights in flames. At the same time, the Kahn's armies march across the plains, breaking his truce and attacking the Arabs. They murder many of them in their sleep.

We watch the beautiful city of Baghdad burn under the starry night on the empty plain. Blood runs in rivers giving the ridges on the dunes a crimson color. Aside from those of us who have wings, we are burned alive. Our cries mingle with those of the Arabs.

***

I lie under the stars, my sunken, hollow eyes gazing up at the constellations. Surely, when the Arabs find me, they will desecrate my dead body. My ghost will wander, restless for eternity.

Now it is my turn to think of the Buddhist prisoner from the Lamastary. I was never afraid of death which I am about to meet. I feel a cold wind, and tomorrow, my soul will feel a scorching sun, an endless eternal desert of torment. My body too will know no rest. It will be defiled, hacked to pieces by Arab scimitars and left to bake in the scorching sun for hyenas and vultures to carry off to their young to gorge.

***

We are a new generation, hatched within hours from the linen uniforms of the dead soldiers. We are born into a harsh reality, a sea of corpses. There is not a living soul to be seen. We have heard the cries of the Kahn's ghost and we take pity on him. Through sand squalls that skirt across the plain, we crawl, emerge from the fabric, and cross the grainy desert making our way to the Khan's corpse, where we have our first meal. Out of compassion, we eat the dead flesh so that his soul may rest.

Escobar's Hippos

The steamy air fogged up the binoculars. Cigar smoke added a green tinge to them that hot, sultry summer's morning as the ghost of Pablo Escobar observed Scarlet Macaws and Multicolored Tanagers flying back and forth in the sunny skies.

Escobar was lying on a lounge chair. His eyes behind their aviator glasses, surveyed the "prison" that the Colombian government had allowed him to build in return for stopping his drug-running actives. Of course, during his life Escobar had broken this promise, but it was not a shabby place to spend the afterlife.

"A full wet bar with marble countertops against sandstone patios running into an infinity pool, what else could you want?" Escobar asked the hippopotamus in the pool who wiggled its ears at the voice it recognized.

"Then there's the gazebo and acre of fruit trees, and don't let me get started about the house. Well, you probably don't want to hear about it anyway since you are not going in there."

The hippopotamus surfaced slowly. The act was truly a graceful one. Its lardaceous body parted the waters gently. This elegance was juxtaposed again a rude, brazen yawn that hippopotamuses are so famous for. The hippopotamus's mouth continued to expand until it was almost at one-hundred-eighty degrees like a protractor, and its ivory teeth glistened in the sun.

"Oh, stop bitching. This place is much better than the enclosure I had built for you at the zoo when I was alive. If you had liked the zoo, you would not have escaped with the others."

The hippopotamus turned around and waved its tail at Escobar as if trying to taunt him.

"You should be glad you are here, you really should. You are the chosen one. It wasn't easy getting you here. Do you know what the government is going to do to you? It is almost as bad as what they did to me when I was assassinated."

The hippopotamus turned around and partially submerged itself, keeping its nostrils and ears above the waterline.

"There are too many of you. There were five when I was alive, now there are seventy. If the government keeps letting you breed, there will be a thousand of you in a decade. They have deemed you an environmental hazard, so they are going to sterilize you.

The hippopotamus surfaced again and yawned.

"I know, I know. It's not fair, I can see your anger by your big yawn. The corrupt government only thinks of itself. The poor people, they consider you an extension of me, of my legacy, now what I am going to do when you are gone?"

"Why do you assume I am angry?" the hippopotamus asked.

"How could you not be? Your manhood is at stake," Escobar said.

"No, I am relieved that someone is cutting the line. I am tired of being associated with a drug lord, with a murderer."

"You are prejudging me," Escobar got up from his lounge chair, walked over to the wet bar, and prepared a gin and tonic.

"How could I be prejudging you?" the hippopotamus asked. "You have been dead for over thirty years."

"Okay," Escobar walked back and lay down on the lounge chair, beginning to sip his drink. I'll give you that. You are post-judging me. Anyway, I have a proposition for you. If I can convince you that my legacy was good, will you agree to go, go deep in the Amazon and reproduce and have the honor of carrying it on? And I'll tell you what, if I can't convince you, I will let you go anyway."

The hippo moved its ears in quizzical figure eights and thought.

"Okay. I didn't choose to come here, and I probably would have been doing what you are suggesting anyway had you not captured me."

Escobar smiled. "Picture this," Escobar took a puff of his cigar, blew a smoke ring and watched a beetle fly through it. "Poor families living in dilapidated houses, with rotting floorboards. The nearest well is five miles away, and they are lucky if they get two hours of electricity a day."

"Doesn't sound very good," the hippopotamus said.

"There's more," Escobar replied, his voice quickening with excitement as he inflated his ego. "The people's material needs are not met, nor are their spiritual ones. The town church: its bell has fallen and is rusty, and it has not been rung in a decade. Termites have eaten all the pews, and there are moths the priest's vestments. Sounds miserable, no?"

"Indeed," the hippo said.

"Now, here's where I come in. With my money, I constructed wells in the village squares, rebuilt the churches and gave them magnificent new golden bells. I had the finest silks imported and gave the priests new vestments, not to mention mahogany wood from Brazil to make new pews. Determined to banish poverty, I demolished the rickety houses and replaced them with sturdy dwellings with reliable electricity. I also built schools in the villages and hospitals."

"Sounds like you turned their lives around," the hippopotamus said. "This is something I could be proud to continue, even if it is only vicariously."

"Well, let me make you even more sure I- "

Crack, crack, crack!

The sound of a gun being fired made the hippopotamus submerge and Escobar flinch. He had not heard the sounds of a firearm for a while, let alone handled one since his death. When no more sounds were heard, the hippopotamus resurfaced, waddled out of the pool, and walked with Escobar to the parapet of the "prison". The pair looked over the wall. On the far side of the bank lay a corpse wearing a policeman uniform.

Escobar then heard the breaking of twigs in the underbrush across the river and spied a man carrying a burlap sack, a small trail of white powder falling out from a hole in it.

"This is your work too," the hippopotamus said quietly. "It's because of this that you were able to revamp houses, reconstruct churches, and dig wells. Those things may have been noble, but they do not outweigh murder. I'm disgusted. I think I'll be going now, but I won't be spreading your legacy."

"I will keep my promise. Let me just go into the house and get my key to the gate. You can start walking to it"

The hippopotamus lumbered toward the gate and took a last yawn as he surveyed the paradise he was leaving. Once at the iron entrance, he looked at the beautiful macaws and tangiers flying around and at the cool Magdalena River.

Crack.

The hippopotamus fell in heap as the bullet entered its brain. Escobar opened the gate and got on his cellphone.

"Come quickly," Escobar said to his associate. "I don't want this beast on my property."

The Margins

Alexander Sergeyevich Pushkin was hopeful when he was summoned to St. Petersburg by Tsar Nicholas I.

The Tsar has been my censor ever since he pardoned me. Perhaps he will permit me to publish my latest poem, "The Bronze Horseman." This was the hopeful thought that ran through the poet's mind as he traveled the several versts by carriage that October. The roads had turned to mud, and the carriage got stuck often.

"Why didn't you order bigger wheels?" Alexander Sergeyevich's wife, Natalia, quipped as she admired herself in a small ivory mirror that she had bought on credit.

"Because I don't have the money, love," Alexander Sergeyevich said, reigning in the sarcasm in his voice. As much as his financial hardships kept him up and caused him to have cold sweats at night, the poet could not find it in himself to chastise his wife. While no one envied Pushkin's debts, almost everyone envied his wife's good looks more than his poetry.

If the Tsar is wise, he will realize the poem serves his regime. The narrative: St Petersburg floods causing much destruction. The Bronze Horseman, a statue of Peter the Great, comes to life to restore order when cursed at by a madman. Not only does the late Tsar restore order and prosperity to the capital, but he also puts the rabble in its place so society can function again.

Not wanting to keep the Tsar waiting, Alexander Sergeyevich had the coachman drive through the night so that they reached the capital by eight o'clock in the morning. Gingerly, the carriage crossed the bridge between Zayachy Island and the center of the city where the Winter Palace was. The river Neva was already frozen.

"What's in that cathedral?" Natalia, Alexander Sergeyevich's wife, asked pointing to the spire on Zayachy Island.

"It's where our blessed Tsars are buried," Alexander Sergeyevich said.

"I hope that one day your poetry graces the Tsar's epitaph," Natalia said.

Alexander Sergeyevich gave his wife a puzzled look.

I already am under so much pressure to satisfy Natalia's material whims. While she is beautiful, she always struck me as shallow. Now I see her opportunism as well.

Alexander Sergeyevich gently rolled up the parchment of his poem and looked out the carriage window at the architecture of the capital.

"What is that statue?" Natalia asked Alexander Sergeyevich, pointing to an equestrian Peter the Great with an outstretched hand trampling a serpent.

"It's the Bronze Horseman," Alexander Sergeyevich said.

"Your latest poem?" Natalia asked.

"Yes, would you like to hear it?" Alexander Sergeyevich inquired.

The pair was interrupted when the carriage came to an abrupt halt.

"State your business," the guard said, chewing on his pipe as he smoked.

"Alexander Sergeyevich Pushkin here to present himself to the Tsar," the coachman replied.

"Ah, His Majesty has been expecting you."

"Yes, I know."

Alexander Sergeyevich opened the window to the carriage. He was breathing hard, and his breath met the frigid air like steam from a locomotive. The poet glanced at his watch. "I believe we are an hour early."

"You had better hurry," the guard said laughing. "The Tsar is expecting you to be at the new Roman Catholic church in the center of town. With the roads in the shape they are in, you will be lucky if you get there fifteen minutes after the hour."

Without saying goodbye to the guard, the coachmen whipped the horses and had them go into a gallop. The abruptness threw Alexander Sergeyevich against the back of the coach, causing the ink on his lap desk to fall onto his copy of "The Bronze Horseman." Alexander Sergeyevich cursed for the rest of the journey. The trio arrived at the church exactly fifteen minutes past the hour.

When the coachman opened the door, Alexander Sergeyevich looked at him smugly and took his wife's hand, denying his servant the honor of escorting her down the steps. The cathedral was massive. Six foreboding gargoyles with bulging eyes and grotesque mouths looked down at the couple as they proceeded through the double doors.

When they entered the building, Alexander Sergeyevich could barely make out the figure of the Tsar standing behind the pulpit conferring with a draftsman. The journey down the nave seemed much longer than it was, and, with each step, Alexander Sergeyevich's heart beat faster. The small figure of the emperor grew larger and larger to reveal Nicholas' huskiness and rough face. True to the soldier he had been, the Tsar had not expected to be in the role he was and had only taken the crown when his older brother had refused it.

"You are late, Alexander Sergeyevich," the Tsar said, looking at his pocket watch. "I am your censor for your poetry, not your movements."

"We thought we were to meet you at the Winter Palace, Your Majesty," Natalia said.

Alexander Sergeyevich looked at his wife with contempt.

Are my writings to be my only correspondence with the Tsar? Can I not speak for myself?

"Never mind your tardiness. Have a seat, Alexander Sergeyevich," the Tsar gestured to a wooden chair with erotic carvings on it. On the sides of the armrests, one could see a naked Pan chasing a voluptuous Syrinx, her breasts accentuated from the red walnut against the mahogany that made up the rest of the structure. On the back of the chair, one could see women engaging in fellatio with men, as they lay under the trestle of a vineyard.

Still reeling from the chastisement of the Tsar, Alexander Sergeyevich did not notice the lewd carvings.

I hope I memorized the poem correctly, as I cannot read it now.

"Do you know what they call that chair?" The Tsar asked.

"No, I do not," Alexander Sergeyevich said.

"That chair is from England. They call it a misericord, or mercy chair, a place where choir monks could rest on rare occasions from the labors of their day and singing God's praises."

Alexander Sergeyevich continued to look vacantly at the Tsar as he tried to temper his anxiety with the recitation of his poem in his head.

"You don't seem phased by the carvings," the Tsar laughed, his barreled chest moving up and down like an accordion. "Perhaps that is because of your womanizing history. No offense to you, Mrs. Pushkin." the Tsar said. "But anyway, the chair was designed this way as the monk who sat on it supposedly kept venal sins in check within the monastery. Just as gargoyles were placed on many religious buildings to spit the sins out of them. Do you have any idea why I summoned you?" The Tsar asked.

"I do not your majesty," Alexander Sergeyevich said. "Although I was hoping it was to discuss my latest work, in the hopes that you would give me the honor and privilege of publishing it."

"Well, let's see it then," the Tsar said. "My business with you can wait until afterward."

"I would read it to you, but unfortunately, I spilled ink on the way here in my coach,"

Alexander Sergeyevich said.

"Pavel," the Tsar called to the draftsman. "Fetch me a piece of parchment, ink, and a quill, and give them to the poet here.

The draftsman, Ivan looked up from the gargoyle he was sketching and fetched the items.

The writer's work is too abstract, so inferior to us artists.

"Write your poem," the Tsar said. "And make sure it is legible."

Alexander Sergeyevich bent down and began to write, his long curls masking his face.

"Did you have a chance to hear your husband's poem?" the Tsar asked Natalia.

"I have not," Natalia said.

Alexander Sergeyevich finished writing, looked up, and asked: "Should I recite it first, your majesty, or read it?"

"Let me read it. Look how long it is," the Tsar said. "And why don't you get up and let your poor wife sit down in that chair and rest herself?

Alexander Sergeyevich handed the Tsar the poem.

This is so humiliating. First, the Tsar had me sit on an obscene chair, and now he has my wife do so. Is he trying to rub salt in the wound? I know every man in St. Petersburg would love to sleep with her.

Alexander Sergeyevich tried to distract himself. He looked around the cathedral. Despite its size, it struck him as crowded with pews, which, as an Orthodox Christian, he was not accustomed to. In Orthodox churches the congregants stood during the services. The presence of statues also baffled him. Still, the craftsmanship of the marble was well done. Alexander Sergeyevich stared at Virgin Mary silently praying to her as he waited for the Tsar to finish reading.

"This poem can be read in two ways," the Tsar said. "It is almost a narrative poem. I see this man, Yevgeny who is trying to escape a flood in our glorious capital. I infer that after the waters of the flood recede, he goes to our city's renowned statue: The Bronze Horseman. He curses my illustrious ancestor, Peter the Great, which brings him to life, and then the statue chases Yevgeny till he dies. You could read this as Yevgeny rebelling against the Tsar or Peter putting Yevgeny in his place as he rides around the flooded city trying to restore order. I trust that I do not have to ask you which interpretation you had in mind?"

"No, Your Majesty, of course you do not. I learned my lesson long ago. All my writing is to praise you and Russia."

"Very good, very good," the Tsar repeated. "Come back tomorrow, and I will give you my answer. Pavel."

"Yes, Your Majesty," the draftsman came running and bowed to the Tsar.

"Take this with you and do what you do best in your spare time," the Tsar handed Pavel the parchment.

Alexander Sergeyevich scowled at Pavel as he took "The Bronze Horseman." Pavel responded with a devious smile.

"Go to the hotel," the Tsar said to Alexander Sergeyevich. "I've reserved a room across from your brother-in-law and sister-in-law. Be back at seven in the morning, and this time do not be late."

Alexander Sergeyevich and Natalia bowed and walked out of the cathedral. Outside a cold rain was falling. Alexander Sergeyevich had forgotten his umbrella, and the gargoyles spat on him and his wife as their spittle was blown in the wind.

"Our churches are so much better," Natalia grumbled, as Alexander Sergeyevich helped her over a puddle and then into the coach.

"To the Romanov Hotel," Alexander Sergeyevich said to the coachman after closing the door.

"I wonder why the Tsar put us up in the same hotel as my sister, Yekaterina, and her husband Georges-Charles D'Anthès?" Natalia said.

"Isn't it obvious," Alexander Sergeyevich replied, glumly. "The Tsar wants to get a rise out of me. Everyone in St. Petersburg from the lowliest porter to the Grand Dukes knows that D'Anthès only married your sister to shake off the true rumors that he has designs on you. Were he not my brother-in-law, I would have challenged him to duel long ago."

The carriage rolled on slowly to the hotel. When the couple arrived, and after they were shown to their room, Alexander Sergeyevich plopped down on the bed, pulled the down cover over himself, not noticing his wife making herself up and leaving.

***

"What was the last thing your husband wrote?" D'Anthès asked Natalia.

"A poem about the statue near the banks of the Neva," Natalia replied.

"The Bronze Horseman," Yekaterina interjected.

"Yes," Natalia said.

"Alexander Sergeyevich sent me a that a while ago. That poem always frightened me," D'Anthès quipped. "When you see Yevgeny go after the deluge and wander around following the Tsar's statue which comes to life, ostensibly trying to restore order. Poor Yevgeny, by the poem's end he is a bloated corpse. To be honest, I think my brother-in-law is living on the margins. It would not shock me if Nicholas bans him from writing like his late brother Alexander did."

Natalia took up her ivory mirror, opened it, and applied some rouge to her cheeks.

"Then I'll be out of blush," Natalia quipped. "My husband's writings are our only source of income."

"But I won't be out, I'll still be blushing," D'Anthès roared with laughter.

Unexpectedly, there was a knock at the door. D'Anthès rose and answered it.

"Pavel, what brings you here?" D'Anthès asked.

"I have something from the Tsar for Alexander Sergeyevich, but the door to his room is locked, so I thought I might give it to you to give to him."

"By all means. His wife, Natalia, is here."

"Please take this," Pavel handed Natalia a cylinder-shaped package. Natalia looked down at the strange box quizzically. "Thank you," Natalia said. Should I wait until morning to let my husband open it?"

"No, the Tsar was hoping that your husband would see it this evening. So please open it and put it in its appropriate space. Once opened you will know where to place it," Pavel replied.

Before Natalia could inquire further Pavel took his leave, hastening to his coach which took off at breakneck speed back to the cathedral.

"I wonder what it is?" Yekaterina said. "Perhaps you should open it."

"No, no," Natalia reported. "The instructions come from the Tsar. I will not open it. But I will be going now. I trust I will see you tomorrow."

"Indeed," D'Anthès said. "Come I will escort you out."

Leaving Yekaterina to wonder what was in the box, D'Anthès walked Natalia to the door and kissed her on the lips just long enough for his wife not to suspect anything. Even though it was only a peck, it was enough to rouse Natalia and cause her face to turn red.

"Even if the Tsar doesn't allow Pushkin to publish the poem, it looks like I won't need blush. Goodnight," Natalia said, kissing D'Anthès on the cheek.

***

When Natalia reached her room, she found her husband in a deep sleep and went to relieve herself, taking the package with her. While in the bathroom Natalia opened the package with the golden string only to reveal a roll of thick toilet paper.

The Tsar is a proper, polite man. What would possess him to send a gift like this to my husband?

Natalia glanced at the toilet paper, only to realize that it was not just any roll. Sure enough, there was her husband's poem "The Bronze Horseman" in black ink. Not only was the poem written in exquisite calligraphy, but the sheets bore images of the entire narrative work, from the commencing of the flood, to Yevgeny's chasing The Bronze Horseman through the streets, to Yevgeny's death. Natalia also noticed that on the edges of the tapestry paper were lewd images similar to the ones on the misericord in the cathedral that the Tsar had had her husband sit on.

I wonder what this means. Is the text of my husband's poem pushing back against the vices of the flesh? Is this a sign that the Tsar intends to let him publish it? Or is it a sign that the Tsar finds it threatening and that it belongs, well, in the toilet?

Natalia then put the roll of toilet paper on the side table next to the toilet and cleaned herself with the regular roll which was in its holder. After washing her hands, she proceeded to the bed. Her husband was still in his clothes. He always wore the same frockcoat and dilapidated shirt. If he did not have his name no one would know that he was from nobility. The estates he'd inherited from his mother were falling apart. Ten years his junior, Alexander Sergeyevich found Natalia shallow, while she found him too frugal for her taste. Natalia lay on her back fantasizing about D'Anthès, her thoughts occasionally disturbed when her husband snored loudly.

***

A few minutes past midnight, Alexander Sergeyevich awoke to answer the call of nature. Clumsily he lit the candle and wandered into the bathroom. Even groggy he was thinking about his poem. Would the Tsar accept it for publication? If he did, Alexander Sergeyevich's career would be resurrected, he would be able to afford things for his wife and climb out of debt. Pushkin grabbed the roll of toilet paper on the side table, finished his business, and went back to bed only to hear his wife talking in her sleep.

"D'Anthès my love, my noble military officer. Ask me to run away with you to Paris, and I am yours," Natalia said turning over on her side.

The words from his wife were too much to bear. Disgusted, Alexander Sergeyevich knew he would not be able to sleep next to Natalia. So, he gathered up his lap desk and some ink from the bedside table and went back into the bathroom. Once there, Alexander Sergeyevich lit a candle and placed it haphazardly on the table next to the toilet paper the Tsar had sent. Alexander Sergeyevich had not managed to write one sentence when he smelled smoke. Looking over his shoulder he saw the flame begin its journey up the paper, and reacted just in time to blow it out, so it had only consumed a corner of a sheet. Alexander Sergeyevich was about to go back to his writing when his eyes wandered back to the roll of toilet paper that had nearly gone up in flames. He looked at it and realized that it was no ordinary roll. Picking it up Alexander Sergeyevich examined it and came to the same conclusion his wife had.

This could be my redemption or my doom. The idea of the roll of toilet paper being a harbinger of his ruin caused Alexander Sergeyevich to feel queasy in his stomach and to have to move his bowels. After Alexander Sergeyevich had relieved himself, an idea popped into his head. Alexander Sergeyevich took the roll of toilet paper with his poem and ripped off the last stanza. After this he returned to his lap desk and scribbled a note.

My honorable brother-in-law D'Anthès,

Please accept the enclosed last stanza of my poem as a gift. I wish to dedicate it to you.

~Yours

A.S. Pushkin.

Carefully, Alexander Sergeyevich wrapped up the paper with the rest of his poem put in his pocket and carried the contents with the end of his work, and the note he had just written, out of his room into the hall. Gingerly, Alexander Sergeyevich walked down the hall and placed the paper under the door with the note before heading back to his room. Once there, he climbed into bed, rolled over on his stomach, and put the pillow over his head trying to ignore his wife's pining for his brother-in-law in her sleep.

***

When D'Anthès awoke with Yekaterina the next morning he did his ablutions and ambled over the door, preparing to go down to the café for his morning coffee, when he nearly slipped on something. Bending down, D'Anthès noticed the note that Alexander Sergeyevich had left him along with the toilet paper. Curious, D'Anthès picked up the contents, read Alexander Sergeyevich's note and then studied the pictures on the paper along with the poem.

So, this is what he dedicates to me. I should hope for his sake the rest is flattering to Russia. After Pushkin meets the Tsar today, I will challenge him to a duel and end this, after which I will return to France, divorce Yekaterina, and marry Natalia.

D'Anthès then went to the café and waited for his wife. Within half an hour she joined him.

"What are we doing today?" Yekaterina asked.

"Paying the Tsar a visit at the Catholic cathedral he commissioned for the French traders."

"Did we receive an invitation?" Yekaterina asked.

"Of sorts," D'Anthès replied.

"Good morning, Georges," D'Anthès heard a voice from behind him only to turn around and see Alexander Sergeyevich holding Natalia's hand.

"Good morning, Alexander Sergeyevich," D'Anthès replied. "Off to the cathedral today I assume?"

"Yes, I hope to see if my poem will be granted publication. Did you get my gift last night?" Alexander Sergeyevich asked.

"I did indeed," D'Anthès said.

"What gift?" Natalia asked.

"Oh, nothing," D'Anthès said with a smile. "Just a draft of a poem."

"I see," Yekaterina chimed in.

"Anyway," D'Anthès began, "we are off to the cathedral too. See you there."

The two coaches departed for the cathedral. The roads were covered with sleet, and they had to go slowly. For the entire ride, Alexander Sergeyevich and D'Anthès stared at each other through their coach's respective windows. Halfway through the journey, the sleet changed to downpouring rain, making the coaches travel even more slowly. When the quartet arrived at the cathedral, the gargoyles were busy spitting out the rainwater.

The four of them entered the cathedral. At the other end of the nave was Tsar Nicholas I, only this time he was not behind the lectern but was sitting on the misericord talking to Pavel.

"Well, what would you do?" the quartet heard Nicholas asking his draftsman.

"I gave it some thought after delivering to Alexander Sergeyevich what you asked me to. The Tsar in the poem punished Yevgeniy to restore order. Yevgeny is a pathetic creature, his following of the Tsar for a year should be read as his trusting in Peter's judgment if not pandering to him. This poem should go to press; it will shore up your authority."

"So be it," the Tsar turned around. "Oh, there you are," the Tsar glanced at his pocket watch. "Not only you are on time today, but you have brought guests. Come, come," the Tsar beckoned the quartet with his hand.

The two couples walked down the nave and bowed to the Tsar.

"I have decided to let you publish your poem," The Tsar began. "I thoroughly enjoyed it and see how it can be of service to the House of Romanov. Did you get what I sent you last night?"

"Yes," Alexander Sergeyevich and D'Anthès said in unison.

Alexander Sergeyevich looked at D'Anthès angrily, but before he could say anything, the Tsar spoke.

"You both did? That's odd. Pavel, did I not tell you to deliver the gift to Alexander Sergeyevich, and no one else?"

"You did, your majesty," Pavel said. "Alexander Sergeyevich was asleep, so I gave it to his wife, who promised to give it to him when she returned from D'Anthès's room."

"And I did return the package as requested. I didn't even open it," Natalia said.

"Interesting," the Tsar mused. "Back to publishing "The Bronze Horseman." It will do for me what the gargoyles have done for this cathedral. It will stamp out sin and treason against me. That is why I sent you the gift. Alexander Sergeyevich, I know you must have been worried sick last night. As I told you before, the poem could have also been read as a criticism of my house."

"Yes, Your Majesty, I am aware," Pushkin replied.

"Very well, that part of our business is settled. Now, I am curious to know how it is that D'Anthès says he got the gift as well?"

"This morning, I found a note penned in Alexander Sergeyevich's hand, as well as this," D'Anthès revealed the toilet paper that was in his pocket.

"Your majesty, I take this as an insult, as you can see it is the last stanza which is a corpse. I consider this an affront and have no choice but to challenge Alexander Sergeyevich to a duel, as he wants me dead."

"D'Anthès, dueling is forbidden if Russia. Should either Alexander Sergeyevich or you engage in one and survive, I will banish you both. You may leave. Alexander Sergeyevich, I suggest you return to your estate to cool off. I will be sure to send you royalties for the publication."

The quartet bowed to the Tsar, walked down the nave, and exited. The gargoyles were now spitting water rapidly.

"I will see you tonight at Chernaya. It is beyond the city limits, so hopefully, we will not get caught. Farewell."

D'Anthès helped Yekaterina into the coach. When her back was turned, he blew Natalia a kiss.

Alexander Sergeyevich and his wife rode back to the hotel in silence.

Natalia will be taken care of if I die. Once back in his room, Alexander Sergeyevich questioned his wife.

"Do you love him? Do you love D'Anthès?" Alexander Sergeyevich asked.

Natalia did not answer.

"That says it all. Well, if I die you will be satisfied on two fronts—that of finances and a husband. I only hope your sister deserts you."

Alexander Sergeyevich spat on the ground. The rest of the afternoon was spent both by Alexander Sergeyevich and D'Anthès looking for seconds, but there were no takers. When D'Anthès tried to say goodbye to Yekaterina she shunned him.

"If you live, enjoy my sister's company," Yekaterina hissed and slammed the door in her husband's face.

D'Anthès met Alexander Sergeyevich outside.

"Whose coach should we take?" Alexander Sergeyevich asked.

"You allowed me to choose weapons. I chose pistols." D'Anthès handed his opponent one. "So, let's have the honor of using your coach."

The coachman helped the two men up, and they started their journey. D'Anthès looked out the window, while Alexander Sergeyevich began to scribble furiously on a piece of paper on his lap desk.

"Another poem?" D'Anthès asked.

"No," Alexander Sergeyevich looked up. "My will."

"How do you know you will die? You have fought many duels."

"I'm just preparing," Alexander Sergeyevich said, glancing at the statue of The Bronze Horseman. Alexander Sergeyevich gazed at the statue and swore it waved at him.

I must be delirious.

The coach arrived at the swampy ground.

Alexander Sergeyevich and D'Anthès each took ten steps back. "You will have to count for us," Alexander Sergeyevich said to the coachman.

"One, two, three," the coachman said.

Crack! The sound of D'Anthès pistol went off, the bullet landing entering Alexander Sergeyevich's upper hip and lodging in the poet's abdomen. Alexander Sergeyevich fell forward and began to cough. The blood from his abdomen began to spurt, staining the will in his pants pocket and making it illegible. Summoning all his strength, Alexander Sergeyevich managed to get up from the mud and get off a shot. But it was not enough, the shot only grazed D'Anthès hand.

D'Anthès walked over to Alexander Sergeyevich and offered his hand. Although his rival was still breathing for a few seconds, it was too late. D'Anthès, with the aid of the coachmen, got Alexander Sergeyevich back in the coach, and they began their journey to the church so the renowned poet could receive last rites.

"Let me at least settle your final wishes, what did your will say?" D'Anthès asked.

"I forgive you."

***

D'Anthès was given the courtesy of being allowed to attend Alexander Sergeyevich funeral. It was held in a small church—not the Winter Palace or the Catholic cathedral. The Tsar feared unrest could rise given the late poet's popularity. After the Mass the Tsar gave instructions for Alexander Sergeyevich's body to be sent off at midnight to his mother's estate for burial, and he made good on his word, banishing D'Anthès from Russia the next day. Natalia did not shed any tears, but Yekaterina cried, and her sobs were not for Alexander Sergeyevich.

***

Alexander Sergeyevich had risen from the grave. Under the light of a harvest moon, he opened the stable doors mounted a horse and rode to St. Petersburg. He passed Zayachy Island where the Tsars are buried, doffed his cap, and rode on.

I'll give them more than an epigraph. The ghost remembered his wife's words when they were last in the capital. Finally, Alexander Sergeyevich could see the outstretched arm of Peter the Great on his horse. He pushed the horse harder until he arrived at the foot of The Bronze Horseman.

"Pyotr Alekseyevich, arise," Alexander Sergeyevich said.

Slowly, the statue moved. The horse Peter was on reared up even further on its pedestal.

"Easy, easy," the former Tsar said to his horse. Then to Alexander Sergeyevich: "Why have you roused me from my slumber? Was there another flood?"

"No. Now get off your pedestal and go survey the city," Alexander Sergeyevich said, taking the toilet paper of his poem out and handing it to the Tsar.

"What is this?" the Tsar asked. "And how dare you speak to me that way?"

"It is a poem in your honor. It has everything but the last stanza," Alexander Sergeyevich replied.

"These drawings are revolting," Peter said.

"Never mind that. Now go!" Alexander Sergeyevich slapped the horse on the hindquarters.

Frightened, the horse galloped for a quarter of a mile before Peter got him under control, but as soon as he did, Alexander Sergeyevich struck it again.

"Would you stop?" Peter hissed. "Were you not already dead, I'd have you consigned to the stocks for a month." But Alexander Sergeyevich would not let up. He chased Peter around the city relentlessly. They passed the admiralty, St Isaac's Cathedral, and eventually traversed the square in front of the Winter Palace.

"Your Majesty, you had better come see this," Pavel said.

"What, what is it? I am busy writing to the press," Nicholas I said. "This had better be important."

"Look! Alexander Sergeyevich is chasing The Bronze Horseman," Pavel said.

"The opposite of what happened in the poem, when The Bronze Horseman chased Yevgeny."

"Do you think this will stop?" Pavel asked.

"God knows," the Tsar replied. "But I am canceling the poem's publication."

The Grander Scuttle

Scapa Flow could not have been more beautiful. Near the horizon, the greenish hues of the Northern Lights illuminated the stark, virtually treeless landscape of the islands. Pussy willows blew in the wind, doffing their catkins to the sky.

In an Italian Chapel, some two kilometers from the Flow, three men sat around a table amusing themselves. One was finishing up a hand of solitaire and the other two a round of dominoes.

"It's still early," Jason said.

"It's not, Jason," Tom said. "You're just not used to the Northern Lights."

"Yes, I know," Jason said while picking up the dominoes. "You know Tom, it's almost as if the sun doesn't want to let go."

"Did it ever?" Jack asked.

"No, I suppose not." Jason took out a small, red plastic barrel from his pocket and unscrewed the lid.

"What have you got there?" Jack asked.

"Just a *Barrel of Monkeys,*" Jason said, pouring out the twelve red plastic monkeys with their signature hooked arms. But Jason didn't *just* have a *Barrel of Monkeys*.

Next to the red plastic monkeys were three white ones from Japan. One covered its ears, another its eyes, and the last its mouth.

"I didn't know we were reverting to childhood," Jack quipped.

"Why did we come here in the first place?" Jason asked, turning in his chair to face Jack.

"To raise the remaining German High Seas Fleet ships scuttled here from World War I," Jason replied.

"Right, and to sell their steel for an immense profit. Scapa Flow is one of the only places in the world where we can find low-background steel that hasn't been exposed to radiation," Jack said.

"Something else that refuses to let go. Radiation has many half lives," Jason said, looking pensive as he tried to pick up a fourth monkey with the three he already linked.

"You're almost a quarter of the way there," Jack said, laughing. "You always have to make things so complicated—always have to challenge yourself and us. Why can't you just learn to enjoy yourself?"

"Lay off," Tom said. "The *Barrel of Monkeys* is his way of practicing operating the winch and chains we need to raise the ships tomorrow. Besides, we've played so much chess and dominoes today that there's nothing else to do. So, if Jason can find a way to occupy himself, more power to him." Tom opened a beer and poured it into his mug.

"Stop defending Jason," Jack said. "He's brought that barrel with him to every wreck we've been to. He knows how to operate the winches by now."

"You guys always tell me to bring something lucky," Jason said. "You always tell me this work is risky business, so this is what I have. Besides, I think this time it wil be different"

"We do," Tom said, filling up Jack's mug with beer. "But after our tenth successful salvaging, I thought you would have outgrown the superstition. I got rid of the photo of my girlfriend.

"You broke up with her," Jason retorted.

"And I left my grandfather's medal for bravery at home," Jack said.

"Hardly something that would look good flashing in Tokyo Bay," Jason replied, smiling facetiously.

Jason glanced outside, the night hidden behind the stained glass, masterfully crafted by Italian war prisoners during World War II. It was hard to admire the Northern Lights.

I don't know whether to be in awe of the craftsmanship or annoyed that I cannot see the Northern Lights. I wonder if the German prisoners felt the same way when they were interned on the ships that the British impounded for their formidability.

"We were in Tokyo. I was on my day off," Jason said, annoyed that the question had gotten him out of his head. He had always loved thinking about how the crews of the various wrecks must have felt just before they went down. This was his way of paying respects to human life.

"I decided to go for a walk and look at the souvenir stalls around the Yasukuni shrine. I found an old man selling the *Three Wise Monkeys*—you know, the ones that hear no evil, see no evil, and speak no evil. The monkeys were cheap plastic ones, not carved of bone. Anyway, I felt sorry for them. I wondered what they were doing around Yasukuni shrine, a place where some of the most heinous Class A war criminals are resting. Were they serving as a warning to others not to repeat history, or were they trying to whitewash it?"

"Let me guess—your mind went with the whitewashing," Tom said.

"Always the pessimist," Jack broke in.

"Would you let me finish?" Jason slammed his empty beer mug on the table. "But you're right. I thought the worst. So, I brought the monkeys and put them in the barrel with the others."

"Why do you still bring it along?" Tom asked.

"Well, every wreck we have been to was caused by war. I guess I just hope that war will end, and the three monkeys I keep in the barrel are the embodiment of that hope."

"Join us," Jack said to Jason.

"No thanks," Jason said, still trying to make his chain of plastic monkeys longer, but still unable to get past three.

"What's the matter with you?" Jack quipped. "You can usually hook around ten monkeys."

"Yes, perhaps that's why we're successful in raising every shipwreck that we have been to so far," Tom said.

"If you guys are so confident, why don't you come over here and try?" Jason asked mockingly.

"We have had three rounds of beer," Tom said. "Surely you can't expect us to do it."

"No, I don't. The heavy lifting is always left to me, "Jason muttered as his friends poured themselves another round and said another toast.

Maybe one day, if I manage to hook all twelve monkeys, wars will stop and all will achieve enlightenment. Not be attached to things, not be human.

***

Jason's three companions went to sleep long before he did.

I knew I should have had some beer too. Then I would be asleep as well. Jason put the red plastic monkeys and the *Three Wise Monkeys* back in the barrel, twisted it closed, then went outside, hoping the cool air would make him tired.

Outside, Jason gazed at the winches lined up along the shore. In the distance, he could see *The Keiser,* the only ship whose funnels still stuck up out of the water. It acted as a memorial of sorts to the Grand Scuttle that Admiral Reuter had ordered.

During the Armistice, the German High Seas Fleet was still nominally German. It was simply interned during treaty negotiations. The British could not board the ships, and while the rules were austere, supplies were sent from home. Because Rueter received four-day late newspapers from the British, he became convinced that hostilities were to resume. Unable to bear surrendering the fleet, he scuttled it.

Jason sat down on the long narrow dock which extended until it was only some seven yards from the ship closest to shore, *The König,* and took out his *Barrel of Monkeys.* First, he lined up the *Three Wise Monkeys* so that they faced the Flow. Then he dumped the red plastic monkeys on the dock and began to hook them. Gingerly, Jason slid the arm of one red plastic monkeys under another, and within a minute, he had four hooked. Things were going well until a gust of wind blew, disintegrating his chain. But Jason wasn't about to give up. For the next three hours he kept trying until he finally hooked all twelve.

"I did it!" Jason screamed into the night as the tide came in and lapped at the shore. Jason packed up the red plastic monkeys and walked toward the church.

I forgot the Three Wise Monkeys. Jason turned around and headed back to the dock.

"He got all twelve," Iwazaru said, uncovering his mouth.

"I know." Kikazaru uncovered his ears.

"This is the first time," Mizaru said as he uncovered his eyes.

"Quick, here he comes," Iwazaru said, covering his mouth. The other monkeys followed suit covering their ears and eyes respectively. Jason gathered the *Three Wise Monkeys*, put them in the barrel, and walked back to the church. When Jason climbed into his sleeping bag, Tom and Jack were snoring like chainsaws. It took a good hour for Jason to fall asleep, but when he did, he was content.

***

"Are they asleep?" Iwazaru asked Mizaru.

"How should I know?" Mizaru replied. "I am the one who sees no evil. I am not about to go and look."

"Would you stop being so paranoid?" Iwazaru protested.

"Stop while you are ahead," Mizaru said. "You are not living up to your name, speak no evil."

"And you two are not allowing me to live up to mine, hear no evil," Kikazaru said, attempting to push his hands around his ears even tighter so as not to hear anything.

"We have to work to together if we are going to live up to our names," Iwazaru said.

"And the only way we can do that is to get Jason to stop opening us up and to let us be. We already were courageous on the dock. We moved our hands for the first time. Why can't we do it again?"

"I still hear snoring," Kikazaru said.

"Fine, I'll look," Mizaru said, twisting open the barrel. "They are asleep."

"Good, let's go," Iwazaru replied.

The *Three Wise Monkeys*, along with their twelve red plastic disciples, hurried outside into the frigid air. They rushed toward the massive winches, their chains resting on the shore. A gentle breeze was blowing.

"I hope the wind doesn't pick up too much," Mizaru said. "That will make the task even harder. Which ship should we raise first?"

"The *Kaiser*," Kikazaru said. "According to Admiral Von Reuter's diary, it was the rowdiest ship."

"And you expect the humans to become enlightened there, of all places?" Mizaru asked. "Imagine being confined to that space for six months with censored news, and no family."

"Well, I don't think we should start with a destroyer. The deck space on those is even smaller," Kikazaru replied.

"Just raise it," Iwazaru said.

The twelve red plastic monkeys turned the winch and lowered the chains. Then they scampered into the cold water, leaving Mizaru, Iwazaru, and Kikazaru to man the crank.

The trio waited for about five minutes.

"Do you think they succeeded?" Mizaru asked.

"We shouldn't have to be doing this," Iwazaru said. "If it weren't for those accursed humans, we could stay in our barrel undisturbed, meditate, and reach enlightenment. They keep reattaching us to the world."

"Well, this might just be our chance," Mizaru said when he felt a tug on the chains. "Quick! Turn the winches."

The *Three Wise Monkeys* quickly set about their work. Iwazaru and Kikazaru grabbed the handles of the winch while Mizaru counted.

"One, two, three, turn. One, two, three, turn," Mizaru said.

Slowly but surely the chains climbed. The first part of the ship to breach the surface was one of the steamers. Then slowly the bow emerged, with the stern bringing up the rear. The dull gray color of the hull could still be seen in some places where debris had not yet breached. The deck railing, covered with seaweed, looked like neglected wrought iron work that one might find in a dilapidated building outside the French Quarter in New Orleans. It was hard to imagine that the workers councils—the communists who had stolen away on the High Seas Fleet—used to dance on these decks, mocking the British soldiers and their officers.

"Just a little more," Mizaru said. By now, the red plastic monkeys were back out of the water, helping to turn the winch until finally the boat was out of the water.

"Should we bring it ashore?" Iwazaru asked.

"No," Mizaru said. "We have to stick to the plan."

They spent the rest of the night repeating the process that brought the *Kaiser* to the surface with three other ships. First, the *König* was raised, then the *Cöln*.

"Now what?" Kikazaru asked.

"We wait," Mizaru said.

"Let's hope tonight's efforts will allow us to live up to our names," Mizaru said as he loosened the barrel's lid so that it could be opened easily before Jason and his colleagues got up.

***

Jason, Jack and Tom walked toward the ships. They expected a long, arduous day of work ahead of them. Raising just one ship, depending on the size, could take several weeks. With one hand in his pocket, Jason twirled the iconic red barrel not realizing it was empty.

"Look! Three are raised already!" Jason said.

"How could that be?" Jack asked.

"Who knows?" Tom started to run to the dock. "Let's get on them before someone else claims them. In this economy, I wouldn't be surprised if the British double-booked permits. I call the *Kaiser*.

Within fifteen minutes, the three men were on the ships. Jack boarded the *König* while Jason commandeered the *Cöln*.

"The poor Germans," Jack shouted. They must have been so cramped. Their ships may have been wider than the British ones, but they weren't designed to be at sea for long periods. Unlike British ships, they had no desalination plants."

"These are some nice viewfinders," Tom yelled. "The British may have had the range, but the Germans' accuracy is what made their fleet so dangerous, even though they were outnumbered."

Jason surveyed the *Cöln*. Of the three ships that had been raised, it was in the best condition. Jason wandered to the officer's cabin, where he found a copy of the positioning of the ships before the scuttle. He also found a mildewy German Navy ensign behind glass that somehow had survived the scuttle. Jason continued to peruse the cabin until he found what he was looking for: the safe where he hoped to find the ship's log.

"Did either of you bring a hammer?" Jason called when he was back on the deck. But he received no answer.

What could the two of them possibly be talking about? Maybe how much money we will have saved.

"Did either of you bring a hammer?" Jason repeated, raising his voice. Still, no answer. Jason looked to his right hand, then left. The other ships were gone! He ran around the other side of the deck only to see the ships being towed out by two tugboats. Jason strained to see who was driving them, but the figures in them were too small.

"Wait to drop your anchors till we tell you," a high-pitched crackling voice commanded through a tugboat's speaker.

"Very good," the voice said. "I don't suggest you try and run; a massive front has moved into the open sea." The tugboats turned around and came toward the *Cöln*. Jason watched in disbelief as red plastic monkeys, under the direction Iwazaru, Kikazaru, and Mizaru, hooked up cables to the *Cöln* and towed it out beside the *Kaiser* and the *König*.

After Jason and the *Cöln* were alongside the other two vessels, the voice from the tugboat speaker spoke again.

"You might as well forget trying to contact help. Your cellphones won't work out here. We are subjecting you to the same conditions the Germans were by the British in 1919. News will be delivered to you four days late. You are not permitted to go ashore. No personal effects may be flown from the ships. Food and water will be brought to you from the lands, but unlike the Germans, since you have no country backing you, you will not be charged for it. Chaplaincy services will be available daily, and your censored mail will be delivered.

"So much for us telling you to give up bringing your good luck charm," Jack chided.

"Never mind that, we are saving tens of thousands of dollars on raising the ships," Tom said.

The three men watched the tugboats headed toward the shore and dropped their anchors.

"Do you think they will come back?" Tom asked.

"Who knows? They are monkeys," Jack answered sarcastically.

The three men tried to pass the time. Jason continued trying to crack the safe without success. Jack sat behind one of the fourteen-inch guns and pretended to fire off into the distance while Tom stared at the church through one of the *Zeiss* viewfinders.

"They are coming!" Tom said.

Sure enough, the monkeys were boarding the tugboats. When they arrived at the three ships, three red plastic monkeys on each ship carried supplies of paper, envelopes, and stamps.

"We will be back in two hours for supper," Iwazaru called over the speaker.

While Jack and Tom still wandered around the ships, Jason accepted the paper.

"Is this some kind of prank?" Jason asked the red plastic monkeys.

"No fraternizing," Iwazaru said over the speaker. The red plastic monkeys turned around and scampered down the sides of the ships to the tugboats.

When the monkeys were gone, Jason tried to make himself comfortable at the damp desk and began composing a letter.

I have to somehow convince the monkeys to tow us back to shore and end this madness. If anyone is going to be able to do this, it is me as I own or at least owned them. Jason closed the cabin door and tried to shut out the loud voices of Jack and Tom. They were going crazy, much in the way the Germans initially did when they were impounded in the Flow.

Jason was only a few lines into his letter when there was a knock at the door.

Which of the buffoons is going to be at the door? Sighing, Jason got up, walked across the small cabin, and opened the door. There at his feet were Iwazaru and Kikazaru, the monkeys who hear no evil and speak no evil respectively.

"Do you have anything to confess?" Kikazaru asked.

"Yes, I wanted—"

"There is nothing I hear that is bad," Iwazaru interrupted. "Remember, I hear no evil."

"And even if you could speak, I would not speak about evil, as I cannot respond in kind," Kikazaru said.

"Then what kind of confession is this?" Jason asked.

"Dinner will be here soon," the two monkeys said in unison, laughing before running to the red plastic monkeys and shimmying down their chain onto the tugboats.

Half an hour later, dinner came. Served on paper plates, it consisted of mashed potatoes, overdone roast beef, and a few wilted string beans. After finishing his meal, Jason went outside to see if he could talk to Jack and Tom. A storm was passing over, and the winds were too strong for his voice to be heard. Discouraged, Jason returned to his cabin and continued his letter to the *Three Wise Monkeys*.

***

Within two days, not only did Jason receive two letters, but the monkeys had wised up. The letters were frantic one-liners from Jack and Tom, asking what the plan was for getting back to shore. They appeared to be uncensored. After all, what could be said that the monkeys and Jason did not already know? The interactions with the monkeys, however, were more interesting. Jason was folding his letters when he heard a knock at the door.

"Is this going to be a repeat of last time?" Jason asked, making his way across the small cabin to the door.

"No, it is not." Jason looked down to see Iwazaru, the monkey who speaks no evil, standing below him. "Listen, Jason." Iwazaru plopped down a four-day-old newspaper. "This is the latest news—"

"No, it's not," Jason cut Iwazaru off. "The paper is four days old."

"This is the latest news you will have access to, just like the Germans in 1919. Now, as I was trying to say before, my fellow monkeys and I have devised a sort of merry-go-round system of communication with you and your friends. I will be the one whom you speak with. Then I will translate what you have said uncensored to Mizaru, the one who sees no evil, will then translate it into a friendly format for Kikazaru, the one who hears no evil. Kikazaru will then translate. We think this system is best as you are not censored in how you speak."

"This is so convoluted," Jason said. "Why have you done this to us, and what do we have to do to get back to shore?"

Iwazaru exited the room and gestured for Jason to close the door. After closing the door, Jason pushed himself up against it, trying to listen to what was being said, but he could not hear anything. Then there was another knock. Jason opened the door, and Kikazaru stood in Iwazaru's place as Jason had been told he would.

"Well, what did you guys decide to tell me?" Jason asked.

"The reason we have sequestered you and your partners is that we want to see what it is like to be human. We are tired of being perfect all the time."

"What is this, some mind trick? I will show you what it is to be human!" Jason raised his voice.

Frightened, Kikazaru pressed his hands to his ears tighter, but the damage had been done. The monkey scampered off. Jason slammed the door behind Kikazaru and went back to his desk. When he sat down, Jason heard a tugboat starting up. He continued writing his letter, hoping that the monkeys would relent and read it at some point.

***

The next day, the storm had let up somewhat, and Jason was able to talk to Jack and Tom.

"How is your monkey business?" Jason asked Jack as he leaned over the railing on the aft of the *Cöln's railing* and lit a cigarette.

"Crazier than ever," Jack said. "This morning, those three monkeys of yours came for their daily chaplaincy rounds or whatever they call it. But they wouldn't just speak to me outright. They had this crazy system where the one that hears no evil had me write down what I wanted to say. Then he took it out and shared it with the one that sees no evil, and the one who speaks no evil delivered a note to me.

"And what did your note say?" Jason asked.

"That the monkeys want to learn how to be human," Jack replied.

"I had a similar experience," Tom said. "Only the one that speaks no evil came and wrote down that he would not speak to me but would only take a note. I wrote one. Then the one who hears no evil knocked on the door and slipped a note under it. I opened the door, but before I could see anyone, the monkeys were gone. I imagine the one that hears no evil wrote it. The note said they wanted to be human."

The bull horn from the tugboats interrupted the three men's conversation.

"Back to your cabins or no dinner," came a voice over the loudspeaker. The three men shrugged their shoulders in bewilderment and went back to their cabins.

***

(Three months later)

Mizaru, Kikazaru, and Iwazaru sat around a small table between the altar and pews in the Italian church. In front of them was a smorgasbord of appetizers. Each monkey nursed his drink of choice while the red plastic ones acted as waiters, pushing around turkey and roast beef carving tables.

"They are getting used to it," Mizaru said, cutting his roast beef and pouring some au-jus on it. "They have even stopped writing letters home."

"I know," Kikazaru said. "It is as if they almost need nothing to subsist. The humans are barely eating."

"We never wanted to have our enlightenment disturbed nor have our barrel opened," Mizaru said.

"And when that could not be accomplished, we decided to see what reality is for most," Iwazaru continued.

"And look, it is backfiring," Kikazaru commented. "The humans are more at peace than us. Besides, where is the barrel, anyway? Maybe now that we have the humans sequestered, we can go back in our barrel without being bothered."

"I think it is still with Jason—unless he gave it to one of his friends. But getting it back will mean confronting the humans," Iwazaru said.

"I am sure when we tell them they are going back to shore, and that they can resume a normal life, all will be fine," Mizaru said.

After Mizaru's comment, the red plastic monkeys slammed on the brakes of the carving tables, causing the food to almost go flying.

"What is the matter with you oafs?" Iwazaru demanded.

"Iwazaru," Kikazaru said. "Remember to live up to your name."

"Well, you are not living up to yours if you heard me," Iwazaru huffed.

"Gentlemen, calm down," Mizaru said, covering his eyes.

***

Jason, Jack, and Tom were on the bows of their respective ships, fishing. It was a cold day, and they were shivering, but they did not seem to mind.

"Gentlemen," came a voice from the loudspeaker. "One of you has the barrel. We have come to retrieve it. Please be advised that within the hour we will be boarding your ships to look for it. Then we will tow you to shore."

"We can't let them do that," Jack said. "I am so used to our routine. Who has the barrel?"

"I do," Jason said.

"Well, just go get it and give it to them. There is no need to interact with the monkeys," Tom said.

"You are right," Jason said. "It's time to take the next step. I found this in the safe." Jason handed Jack and Tom a journal with blueprints in it.

"It's the plans to the seacocks," Jack said.

“Our chance to be free from the wheel of life,” Tom said.

“We have a good hour before they get here. Look! There are clouds over the horizon,” Jason said.

As the storm clouds opened up, the red plastic monkeys’ smiles turned to frowns.

“What are you frowning at?” Iwazaru demanded.

“Iwazaru, must I remind you again? Kikazaru asked.

“Look! Look!” Mizaru exclaimed. “The German ships are sinking! I am not supposed to see this! Quick! Go faster! We have to get the barrel!” Now the storm was picking up. The *Kiaser* was on its side, the *König* stern was starting to lean, while the *Cöln* was doing the same, only bow side.

***

Jason felt something cold on him.

“Wake up! Wake up!” Jack said, throwing another pail of water on Jason. “Did you have more to drink than we did last night?”

“What, what’s going on?” Jason stammered. “Did the ships go down??”

“We are not dead, and we could be coming back to another life full of riches if things go right, come on,” Tom said, helping Jason to his feet. Jason got up and then felt something fall out of his pocket. He looked down only to see his *Barrel of Monkeys*.

“Don’t tell me you are going to take that with you,” Jack said.

“No, don’t worry. I am not,” Jason said, picking up the barrel.

"Then why are you taking it with you?" Tom asked.

"You'll see," Jason said.

The trio went outside. It was a sunny day, but one that would only last for about six hours given the season.

"Here's to raising the ships!" Jason cried, throwing the sealed *Barrel of Monkeys* as far as he could into the Flow.

"Well at least we won't be disturbed," Mizaru said. "I won't see any evil."

"And I won't hear any evil," Kikazaru said.

"And now, free from all humans, I'll have none to speak of," Iwazaru said as the tide carried them out of the Flow of the high seas—to the internment they had always dreamed of.

The Golden Goosestep

"My life has always been determined by the course of history, not by me."
–Alfred Krupp

1871

These were the words on King Ludwig II's mind when he penned his letter to the Kaiser:

It is a tragedy that I must lose my kingdom and be king only in name, but at least now I can focus on promoting my beloved Wagner and building my castles.

As Ludwig affixed his seal, he tried to forget about Bismarck's threats to blackmail him and expose his preference for men. With a heavy sigh that made the front locks of his hair rise like a choir upon the arrival of the conductor, Ludwig gave the letter to the page. And just like that, Bavaria was incorporated into the Second Reich and Germany was founded.

***

The horses strained under their harnesses as they crossed the Ruhr. There were a dozen of them, but still their load was heavy. A canopy of trees provided some welcome shade while walking the last mile to the factories at Essen. A May breeze blew the nascent blossoms off the trees causing them to fall on the shiny, oblong, metal load they were carting behind, like a troop of mourners bidding farewell to some emperor or statesman.

But this was no goodbye. As soon as the horses and their driver rounded the bend a chorus of cheers could be heard from men—with their coal-stained faces from working underground in the mines, or premature wrinkles from the steel mills—standing on the muddy, saturated ground singing: *Hiel di rim Sigerkranz*[7]. Above the men dressed in a suit stood the owner of the metropolis of Essen and its massive, gargantuan steelworks: Alfred Krupp. A burly man with pudgy hands, a ruddy face and somber gray eyes. Alfred doffed his bowler hat as the fruits of his labor passed. Once the cannon had been sequestered in its shed the men turned and faced their leader who cleared his throat and began to speak.

"Gentlemen, some of you have been here twenty-five years, some of you fifty. Some of you long enough to remember when we as a firm only produced rail ties, wheels for trains, and yes, spoons. I remember some of you coming to my house, complaining how the Austrians prefer thinner spoons, with a wider bowls, while the French have a liking for thicker handles and

7 Hail to Three in the Victor's Crown

are averse to apostle sets as they had shed all religious undertones since their revolution seventy years ago.

I have news for you. Yes, we will continue to produce rail ties and train wheels as that is what helped us move our troops quickly to win this war. But we will no longer produce spoons. No longer will we try to decipher the language of individual tastes. Rather, we will focus our energies on distance our neurosis on cannons, and weapons of war, a language all cultures understand. Germany deserves its place in the sun."

Another cheer went up. Alfred acknowledged it, but when it went on for more than thirty seconds, his grin abruptly turned into a frown. He was highly punctual and had only budgeted five minutes from his speech.

"Gentlemen," Alfred's voice boomed. "That is quite enough, now back to work. Make sure the last deliveries of spoons goes out. From then on only produce cannons and railroad items. I sense that within fifty years, we will be at war again.

The men turned around and marched in columns like ants back to their mines leaving Alfred alone. Once the men were out of sight, Alfred walked across the muddy ground in his jackboots to the shed where the cannon was stored.

The door grudgingly gave way when Alfred pushed it, causing him to huff in dismay as it had not been oiled in a timely manner. There, in the corner of the shed was Alfred's steel cannon glistening in the sunlight. To the casual observer one might have mistaken it for silver as it had been so meticulously polished after the victory in France.

"I have done as you asked, Hans." Alfred began. "From now on—"

"I should be in Paris, marching down the Champs–Élysées, past the Eiffel tower." Hans turned around from his sulking baring his muzzle threateningly at Alfred. "If I had shells in me, I'd shoot you. How dare you emasculate me, deny me the honor of complete victory."

"Hans!" Alfred raised his voice. "It wasn't me. Had I been in command we would have overrun all of France. You have no idea how elated I was when I got the cables from Berlin that you were shelling the center of Paris from over ten miles from the city's limits. It was Bismarck's and the Kaiser's decision."

"So, from now on you will only manufacture items of war, or those that can be used for war?" Hans asked his tone becoming more mellow.

"Yes, as soon as I get the influx of cash from Berlin, I will begin just making weapons. The last order of spoons goes out tomorrow, and the remaining stock I will melt down."

"We should start making cannons now, not wait for the bureaucracy of Berlin." Hans said.

"But I need the capital." Alfred protested.

"Find another way!" the cannon awkwardly shifted himself, so his muzzle again faced the corner of the shed and sulked.

However, the money for Berlin was to come sooner than expected. Soon, the whole factory was producing rail ties and wheels as ordered by Berlin for the next war. It would take fifteen years until the order changed for just strictly armaments, and fifteen years for Alfred Krupp to remember to mail his last set of spoons (Apostle spoons) to his client Ludwig II of Bavaria.

***

FIFTEEN YEARS LATER
1886

Ludwig's ghost shuffled around the long oak table of Singers Hall at Neuschwanstein Castle.

"You have kept us waiting for fifteen years," a haggard ghost dressed in an old Prussian Blue uniform with a bandaged forehead said.

"Did you have to wait until you yourself were dead?" another ghost of a soldier with a missing leg and a body which had succumbed to gangrene asked. "Maybe you really are crazy. Maybe the psychologist the Bavarian parliament hired who deemed you insane without ever seeing you was right.

"And maybe it was because you act like a looney that you drowned the psychiatrist and committed suicide," the first solider said. "And that was only yesterday."

Ludwig ignored the peanut gallery, and opened one of the massive oak cabinets. He took out a velvet case.

"Ah, here they are!" Ludwig exclaimed, his face breaking out into a smile to reveal his dimples. "I was so excited to get them yesterday I forgot where I had put my spoons. They arrived from the Krupp factory in Essen yesterday, a whole fifteen years late. And gentleman, I will have you know, that is why I am so late in serving you. Ludwig took out the spoons and placed them by the ten men's bowls and then served them the foie gras soup."

The ghosts of the men looked wide-eyed at the delicacy, and some moved their spoons to dip in.

"Ah, ah, not yet," Ludwig admonished the men. "We still are waiting for a few more guests. As you can see some seats are still vacant."

"So do we have to wait another fifteen years?" the man with the maimed leg asked.

"Perhaps, I do not know when the others we are expecting will turn to ghosts, and join us," Ludwig replied.

"Maybe the psychiatrist didn't deem you insane for bankrupting Bavaria with all these castles you built," the man with the injured head mused.

"Perhaps not," the amputee said. "Perhaps it was for another reason. We all know you *like men*."

"And?" Ludwig said. "Love is love and good deeds are good deeds. And bad deeds are bad deeds. Now, why don't you gentlemen compare spoons to see what apostles you got."

"I have John," one of the men said.

"And I Luke," another said.

"Does it matter," a third chimed in. "They all would disapprove of Ludwig."

The men laughed in unison.

***

1887

"Is my child almost ready?" Hans asked excitedly when Fredrich Krupp came into the shed. Fredrich wore all black and was looking sullenly at the floor.

"What's the matter?" Hans asked. "Is the Kaiser cutting funding? Do you have to close the Krupp firm that has been in the family for ten generations? You look as if you have been to a funeral."

"I have, Hans," Fredrich said. "Alfred is dead. I just buried him."

"My condolences," Hans said tenderly. But then unable to contain himself, he went back to his usual bombastic tone. "So, what's the update with the new cannon, my new child?"

"The Kaiser has now told us to produce half the railroad implements we have been, which frees upon funding for cannons, but it's not enough in its own right," Fredrich said.

"Find another way!" Hans shot back repeating the same words he had said to Friederich's father over three decades before.

"I have, calm down," Fredrich said. "I just signed an agreement with our competitor in Great Britian, Vickers. In return for Krupp shells, which work with their cannon, for every man killed in battle in any of Britain's wars, we are to receive four Marks."

"Wonderful!" Hans exclaimed. "Those imperial British, their Empire is always at war with someone."

"Exactly," Fredrich said. "Let's just hope Germany is not at war with Great Britian anytime soon."

***

1913

The miners with their coal-covered faces, and the steel mill workers with their premature wrinkled faces, were all assembled outside for the first time in thirty-four years, with Gustav Krupp von Bohlen und Halbach, Friederich's son-in-law who had taken over the Krupp firm upon his death.

As soon as Kaiser Wilhelm II's motorcade pulled up under the gray soot-stained sky, there was a rapturous shout from the crowd, and they burst out singing:

"Hiel di rim Sigerkranz!"

The Kaiser, with his trademark, thick, walrus-like moustache which curled at the ends waved, got out of his car. He took care to hold his withered right arm (which had been disfigured after a difficult birth) behind his back.

Gustav Krupp von Bohlen und Halbach came down from the podium and met the Kaiser. Bowing and then shaking his hand hardily. The Kaiser then ascended the podium where Gustav Krupp von Bohlen und Halbach had been and addressed his subjects.

"Loyal subjects of the Black Imperial Eagle," the Kaiser began. "Once again, the storm clouds of war hang over the continent. We face encirclement form France, Russia, and Great Britain. Therefore, I am counting on you to produce cannons. Hence forth, you are only to produce cannons and shells, as well as guns. The Second Reich is counting on you. Germany's prosperity lies in the Ruhr, and nowhere else!"

An electrifying cheer whet up from the crowd. Then the Kaiser walked off the podium to tour the factories with Gustav Krupp von Bohlen und Halbach.

***

"My most sincere condolences on the death of your father-in-law," Kaiser Wilhelm said as he pinned the Order of Black Eagle Second Class on the suit of Gustav Krupp von Bohlen und Halbach. "He was a great man. It is because of the artillery, and the cannons he produced that we were able to defeat the French so quickly at Sedan. Your factory seems to be humming along splendidly, almost like clockwork. Before I go, do you mind if I look at old Hans?"

"Not at all, mien Kaiser," Gustav Krupp von Bohlen und Halbach, replied. "It would be my pleasure."

The door to the massive shed opened easily this time, as it had been well oiled, causing Gustav Krupp von Bohlen und Halbach, who had inherited his father-in-law's perfectionist tendencies, to smile.

"Here he is, old Hans himself." Gustav Krupp von Bohlen und Halbach pointed to the dimly lit corner where old Hans looked a little rusty despite being cast from stainless steel.

"Gustav Krupp von Bohlen und Halbach," the Kaiser said walking to the back of the shed and caressing the canon's muzzle. "I'm surprised at you. Here you are running a first class, or should I say world-class factory, and you neglect to polish Hans, the very entity that caught Berlin's attention and for that matter my treasury's."

"I am sorry, I just—" Gustav Krupp von Bohlen und Halbach began before being cut off by the curt Kaiser.

"No excuses. Now tell me about the next generation of cannon." the Kaiser said.

"Well, for one this artillery piece will have the unheard-of range of nearly twenty-five miles. With this fire power it should be able to conquer France. We can even hit Dover from the other side of the English Channel..." Gustav Krupp von Bohlen und Halbach explained before being cut off.

"We will conquer France, have no doubt about it," the Kaiser broke in.

"And what is more, this cannon will be able to be transported by rail. It will be moved in two parts so it can easily be put back together on the battlefield," Gustav Krupp von Bohlen und Halbach finished.

"Excellent!" the Kaiser exclaimed. "And have you a name for this weapon?"

"But of course," Gustav Krupp von Bohlen und Halbach said. "Bertha, after my wife."

The Kaiser frowned. "What is happening to my Reich? It is modernizing so quickly, and while this is good. Soon we will be the greatest power in Europe. Who ever heard of a cannon being named after a woman. I will let you name it after a woman on one condition."

"Anything mein Kaiser," Gustav Krupp von Bohlen und Halbach replied. "I'll do anything."

"Very well. You should know that when you were just a little boy, I was told by your late grandfather-in-law that he would never allow two things to happen to this firm. One, it would never be run by a woman. And two, no matter how bad things became financially, Krupp Steel would never be turned into a publicly traded company. I trust you will keep this promise made by your late grandfather-in-law."

"Not only will I keep it in honor of him. Gustav Krupp von Bohlen und Halbach said. "But I will do it to honor my living Kaiser. May Alfred rest in peace."

"Excellent, and now I take my leave." the Kaiser turned around and left the shed, leaving Gustav Krupp von Bohlen und Halbach with Hans.

"You intend to name my child after a woman!" Hans bellowed. "What has come over you?"

"Hans, I love my wife..." Gustav Krupp von Bohlen und Halbach said.

"And I love my country!" Hans shouted spiting the residual aged gunpower from his muzzle into Gustav Krupp von Bohlen und Halbach's face.

"You'll see a birth in a month!" Gustav Krupp von Bohlen und Halbach said turning around and stomping off.

"I don't want to see her! I hope she explodes on the battlefield like an obsolete bronze cannon!" Hans shouted back.

***

The soldiers mocked Bertha as they wheeled her to the train.

"Be gentle," Bertha said as they undid her nuts and bolts and split her in two. "Hey watch it!"

"Sorry my fräulein," a captain said sarcastically. He pushed her muzzle backwards and closed the freight car doors. Then he slammed the doors shut.

Bertha was nervous as the train rode through the night. The soldiers could be heard in the passenger cars and the coal car, which was serviced by Ruhr coal singing:

Deutschland, Deutschland über alles[8]...

8 Germany, Germany, above all.

When they arrived at the front some twenty miles outside Paris, the team of soldiers set Bertha up faster than they had unassembled her in the Ruhr.

"Women should not complain and know their place," a colonel said, wiping sweat from his brow as he tightened the last bolt connecting Bertha's muzzle to the rest of her body.

After Bertha was assembled, a general walked to her back and looked in the viewfinder.

"I must say Herr Krupp von Bohlen und Halbach outdid himself. The viewfinders are better than those of Zeiss which are installed on the U-boats. Why, I can hit the Eiffel Tower!" The general said.

"Don't do that, I think the Kaiser will be upset. He wants us to march past it when we conquer France," a private said, pulling the skin on his face while shaving and using the gleaming steel of Bertha as a mirror.

"Attention," the general shouted, causing the private to look up with a start and nick himself with his razor. "To your stations!'

The men ran to their stations. One yoked the horses, while another guided them. A third operated the crank to position Bertha.

"Three degrees right, forty-five degrees high," aim right at central Pairs... Fire!" the general yelled.

Boom. Bertha jerked back. Her teeth banked against each other as she expelled the gargantuan shell. Reems of gunpowder spittle ran down her, but the target was hit.

"*Wunderbar!*[9] Again!"

"*Jawohl*[10]," the private said adjusting the viewfinder.

9 Wonderful!
10 Subservient form of 'yes'

"Wait! Wait!" the general looked up with his binoculars. I see a flock of pigeons. Let's take them out with our new breech loaders. The men jumped form their stations and lined up next to the general. Then opened fire on the defenseless birds.

"Perfect," the general said as the birds fell around Bertha, the letters they carried exposed by the breeze. Bertha looked down to try to get a glimpse of them.

Are they love letters to the front? If only anyone cared about me.

But Betha's thoughts were quickly interrupted as she was loaded up again and fired. This time, the gunpowder ran over her eyes leaving her unable to see if her target had been hit. A cheer erupted form the men confirming that she had done her duty.

***

It looked like the Germans might take Paris, but the French drafted every taxi in the capital and rushed fresh troops to the front. Then, trench-warfare set in, and the war dragged on. Everything, even spoons for eating became scarce. When it became apparent that the war was lost, Gustav Krupp von Bohlen und Halbach began to convert his factory into peacetime operations, and began to send spoons to the front. They were the various spoons different monarchies had requested, the regal apostle spoons he had sent to King Ludwig II some forty years before.

"What are we doing? Why are we manufacturing spoons?" thew foreman asked when Gustav Krupp von Bohlen und Halbach toured the factory.

"The war is lost," Gustav Krupp von Bohlen und Halbach sighed. "The Kaiser and the High Command may not be able to admit it to themselves, but it is true. Should there be peace, there is no way we are going to be allowed to make armaments. But we are a firm, and we must go on, my grandfather-in-law was promised that we would never turn into a publicly traded stock company. So, if we must make spoons, so be it."

***

In mid-November, shortly after the armistice was signed, two-dozen horses struggled as they crossed the Ruhr pulling Bertha in their wake. She was sooty and haggard. A layer of dirt adorned her from being kicked up by the Clydesdales. There was no welcome from the trees on either side of the road, no confetti of spring blossoms, no tickertape parade. The trees had shed their most of their leaves. A few dead ones clung to their branches like mourners.

When the horses, men, and Bertha rounded the bend, there was no throng of coal miners and factory workers to greet them, only Gustav Krupp von Bohlen und Halbach himself. When the throng reached him he had six words for them.

"Put the cannon in the shed."

***

"I knew you were useless," Hans chastised his daughter.

"I did all I was supposed to, not a target was missed," Bertha protested.

"Ah, but you were unable to keep the men's moral up!" Hans shouted. "That's why we lost the war. Had a man been in charge—"

"It had nothing to do with the men's will, it had to do with mine. I did not want the war—" Bertha began.

"I rest my case," Hans said with a huff. "I knew you would be nothing with your disfigurement."

"But I hit all the targets," Bertha said.

"The Kaiser may have been disfigured too, he had a limp arm, but he never gave up," Hans said.

"But he did, he fled to The Netherlands," Berta said. "Didn't you hear?"

"How could I hear anything from this shed? Get used to it you are not going to hear anything either," Hans said.

***

1886

The men were still seated in the Singers Hall of Neuschwanstein. The stunning murals of Wagner's opera, Tannhäuser. On the mural were dancers and beautiful swimming swans, Ludwig's symbol. None of this was of interest them anymore. Even the ghosts of more recent arrivals, ghosts of the dead from the First World War, were bored.

"Why did you pick the swan as your symbol?" the man with the maimed leg asked as he lit his pipe and blew smoke rings out of boredom. "I see it everywhere."

"Because I am the Swan Knight. If anyone asks my name, I disappear, like the Swan Knight in the opera."

"Your name is Ludwig," the man with the bandaged head said.

"You all may know my name," Ludwig said walking across the massive hall to answer a knock at the door. "But I am not in love with you. Only if I tell the one I am in love with, will I disappear, and never see them again."

"I wonder who that is," the amputee said.

"Probably all of us. Hey Ludwig, when are the other guests coming? It's been years, and my soup has gotten cold."

"Thank you," Ludwig said to the courier. Ludwig walked back over to the large oak table, and opened the package to reveal spoons. They were not regal like the apostle spoons and were smaller. Ludwig distributed them to the men.

"More spoons," the men sighed in unison.

"Yes, dessert spoons," Ludwig said, smiling.

***

1933

Gustav Krupp von Bohlen und Halbach was growing old. His armaments had not been enough to win World War I, but he had accomplished one thing: He had sired a son, Alfried named after both his grandfather, Fredrich, and great-grandfather Alfred. Things were also looking up for Germany. A new leader, Adolf Hitler, had come to power. His public works had ended the depression, and he was preparing for war. Once again Gustav Krupp von Bohlen und Halbach was making cannons.

"This one will be even bigger than Bertha," Gustav Krupp von Bohlen und Halbach showed Alfried his blueprints. "Not only has Berlin been generous with its funds, but I threatened to take Vickers to court, and we settled for two marks for every person killed by Krupp shells in pervious wars before The Great War, so we have plenty of money."

***

"I sense I am to become a mother and you a grandfather," Bertha said to Hans.

"And what makes you say that?" Hans whispered. The old cannon was rusting and falling apart. He was dying. Bertha, out of the goodness of her heart had found old spoons and was feeding him some ancient gunpowder she had found in a barrel.

"Haven't you heard the hammers clanking more lately, and the radio of Hitler saying there will be war—"

Bertha's talking to her father was cut short when the door opened, and a team of horses dragged a gargantuan artillery piece into the shed. It was four times the size of Bertha and some ten times the size of Hans.

"Hans, Bertha, congratulations on the birth of your grandchild and child. Meet Gustav!" Gustav Krupp von Bohlen und Halbach, smiled as he spoke. "This is the cannon that will take down Pairs, and God willing Moscow.

"He's adorable," Berta beamed, inching forward to hug the artillery.

"At least he is a boy!" Hans said.

***

Like World War I, World War II initially went well for the Germans. Poland and France fell is short order. The men were told that they would be home by Christmas. Gustav had taken down Pairs and was now going to the Eastern Front.

Moscow was saved in 1941, and Gustav had been transferred to take the Black Sea port of Sevastopol, which was putting up a spirited defense.

"Quit writing letters to home, and load another shell. We will take Fort Stalin soon," the General barked at his crew.

"They have been holding out for weeks," a captain protested. "While the shells do penetrate the reinforced concrete it takes an hour to load each shell. The artillery is so big."

"Well, what do I have to do to motivate you? The Führer demands that the city be taken by end of the month."

"Let me name this artillery. Dora," the private replied.

"I beg your pardon," the General said, removing his glasses and look at his subordinate perplexed.

"You heard me, let me name this artillery piece Dora, after my love at home in Bonn. It will motivate me to have her fight by my side."

"Fine, whatever you need to get you to take the city," the General said, returning to his bunker to direct operations.

Gustav, who had been sworn at, kicked, and told to buck up by the soldiers, was now treated with love. Between every shot they polished him, or maybe her, or both, or perhaps none at all. No longer did the artillery spittle gunpowder after every shot. They were quickly wiped, and for the rest of the war they could see the city clearly, and the progress they made. They also saw the way the soldiers behaved after the city was taken.

Soviet soldiers were beaten gratuitously. The few women amongst them were subject to rape, and humiliation, before they were sent to camps. Some to Gustav Krupp von Bohlen und Halbach's factories in the Ruhr.

***

1945

Gustav Krupp von Bohlen und Halbach fled to Schloss Blühnbach in the Austrian Alps with his wife Bertha.

"It's over; it's over. There will be no more chances!" Gustav Krupp von Bohlen und Halbach cried from a rocking chair in the living room of the late Archduke Franz Ferdinand's hunting lodge the couple had purchased a few decades before.

"Gustav, Gustav, calm down," Bertha counseled, holding a wet towel over her husband's forehead.

"How can I be calm!" Gustav Krupp von Bohlen und Halbach shouted growing red. "How can I be calm when I am surrounded by animals on the walls, shuddered of them. The bears are baring their teeth, the wolves look as if they want to devour me, the eagle's talons are spread as if they want to carry me up by my neck to their nest and feed me to their young."

"Gustav, relax," Bertha said. "The animas are dead they are the late Archduke's hunting trophies. The animals you see are dead!"

"But the Russians are not! If they find me here, they will brand me a war criminal and hang me at the noose with Hitler!"

Gustav Krupp von Bohlen und Halbach's antics were interrupted by the sound of a huge flock of geese flying overhead. The cacophony of sound was so loud that Bertha stepped out on the balcony to look at them. Mile upon mile of geese flew by. Their honking grating to the ears.

"My armaments used to be as numerous as these geese, and they have proven to be my golden gooses!" Gustav Krupp von Bohlen und Halbach wailed as the moon rose.

***

1945
Nuremberg

Gustav Krupp von Bohlen und Halbach's senility has prevented him from standing trial. But this did not prevent the allies from having his son take his place on the stand. As the war had dragged on, Alfried had taken over many operations, and had been involved in overseeing forced labor he specifically requested come from Auschwitz.

Alfried Krupp listened on his headphones as the star witness Gustav/Dora gave testimony against him.

"After the siege of Sevastopol was completed, I was shipped back to the Ruhr to be refitted and maintained," Gustav/Dora began.

"And what did you see while you were there?" the prosecutor asked.

"The prisoners were very badly clothed during the year and half I was back in the Ruhr. I never saw them given new clothes which were suitable for the winter," the artillery said.

"Did you see any forms of overt mistreatment? What you describe is neglect, was there anything else?" the prosecutor asked, pacing in front of the witness stand as he adjusted his monocle.

"Yes, the wives of the workers were trained to beat the prisoners with whips to make them work. One of the foremen would make pregnant women stand, or should I say crouch, as there was no room to stand in the locked cubicle while he poured ice-cold water on top of them in the dead of winter."

"No further questions your honors," the prosecutor said to the three judges—one from each of the victorious Allies took their seats and gestured to Gustav/Dora after that/they were done testifying.

The spectacle of dragging the artillery out of the court room was comical. Four-score of horses were needed.

When the artillery was gone, Alfried took the stand.

"How do you address the charges of destruction of private property in war?" the prosecutor asked, rising from his seat.

"I would like to say, that in terms of the charges of destroying private property at war, I was under orders from Hitler. Had I not compiled, I would have found myself in a camp," Alfried began. "I was just following orders."

"And to the charge of injuring enemy civilians with your armaments?" the prosecutor asked.

"I myself did not fire my weapons; the crews were trained in how to use them. If indeed civilians were harmed, it was not by my negligence. Things happen in the fog of war," Alfried replied.

"Quite right, some of the shells the British used also bear your name," the prosecutor said.

"As to the charge of slave labor?"

Alfried was silent.

"As to the charges of slave labor?" the prosecutor asked again, more forcefully.

Alfried remained silent.

"No further questions, your honor," the prosecutor said.

***

1957

On a misty morning, as Ludwig's ghost drove in his car to Schloss Blühnbach, to belatedly thank Gustav Krupp von Bohlen und Halbach for the spoons. He also intended to call upon Bertha, as he had heard Gustav Krupp von Bohlen und Halbach was mortally ill. As he rode, Ludwig read the paper.

Alfried Krupp sentenced to twelve years in prison for crimes against humanity.

Meanwhile, coming from Nuremburg, and drawn by forty-eight horses, was Gustav/Dora. They had hired a team with the last of their marks. They had even sold some of their leftover shells—soon to be collector's items, no doubt—to raise capital.

"Germany will liberalize, it will have to after this war," Gustav/Dora said to the driver as they crossed the border into Austria.

"No doubt if it wants friends it will have to," the driver said. "Within six decades, we will be one of the most liberal countries in all of Europe. Same-sex marriage will be legal, there will be a thriving LGBT scene, and we will again be at the head of Europe economically."

"I hope so," Gustav/Dora sighed. "But I am afraid I am a bridge too far, at least for now. Who can accept an entity that does not identify as either sex?"

"Indeed, indeed," the coachman said thoughtfully. "If that is not against nature, I don't know what is."

***

Ludwig and Gustav/Dora arrived at Schloss Blühnbach at the same time. They paid their drivers and made their way to the entrance door.

"After you," Ludwig said.

"No after you," Gustav/Dora said, bowing their muzzle.

"Yes, and who might you be?"

"Gustav/Dora, the latest and the last cannon piece that will ever be produced in the Krupp factory, and that's a good thing," the artillery piece said matter-of-factly.

"Is it?" Ludwig asked, entering the hunting lodge.

Is it? Of course it is! Who wants weapons of war on this earth? Gustav/Dora thought.

"Your majesty!" Bertha exclaimed, getting up from her ottoman beside the rocking chair where she had been nursing Gustav Krupp von Bohlen und Halbach.

"Bertha!" King Ludwig embraced the wife of his old patron. "Why are you here? I came as soon as heard of your whereabouts."

"They initially wanted to put Gustav Krupp von Bohlen und Halbach on trial. Thank God they did not. My poor husband, he is so senile he cannot remember half of the war. I trust you heard of what happened to our son?"

"I did," Ludwig said. "I almost didn't come to thank you for the spoons you sent as I thought you would be too upset."

"Oh, don't be daft, any company is welcome. Come sit down, can I get you some tea?" Bertha asked.

"Please," King Ludwig replied.

"I'll have some too please," Gustav/Dora said.

Bertha looked up and nearly dropped the teapot.

"Good gracious. What is that?" Berta asked.

"Bertha, relax." Now it was Gustav Krupp von Bohlen und Halbach's turn to console his wife. "I know that artillery. It is Gustav, named after me."

"Gustav/Dora," the artillery corrected Gustav Krupp von Bohlen und Halbach.

"Gustav/Dora?" Gustav Krupp von Bohlen und Halbach sat up abruptly. "How can you be named after two people? And how can you be two sexes at that? I knew Germany was becoming more liberal, your mother served at the front in World War I, and we all know the rumor that the King here has a shine for men, but two genders? What is this world coming to? Bertha, let the artillery stay as he or she or whatever it is, they are the pinnacle of my craftsmanship. I—" Gustav Krupp von Bohlen und Halbach fell back and collapsed.

"Gustav! Gustav!" Bertha cried dropping the tea pot so that it shattered. "Call an ambulance!" Bertha screamed "The lines were just reconnected."

Ludwig immediately phoned the nearest village. "Send an ambulance right away Gustav Krupp von Bohlen und Halbach appears to have suffered a heart attack."

***

Ludwig's efforts at CPR were fruitless, and the ambulance took fifteen minutes to come. Despite his efforts, Bertha would not allow him to accompany her and her husband, leaving the King alone with the artillery.

"What brought you here?" Ludwig asked Gustav/Dora.

"I had to get out where no one can see me," Gustav/Dora said with tears their eyes. "You saw how Bertha treated me. I am an outcast."

King Ludwig came and touched Gustav/Dora on the muzzle.

"I know how you feel. I am one even in my own house. The men there, who dine at my table...they mock me."

"My sympathies." Gustav/Dora awkwardly rolled themselves outside onto the massive balcony and took aim at a flock of geese with some buckshot, killing a dozen instantly.

"What was that for!" Ludwig exclaimed "I know you are upset, but to take it out on innocent birds?"

"They are my golden geese," Gustav/Dora replied. "Before I left the Ruhr, when it became clear we were losing the war, I made deal with the men. For every goose I take down and send them as food, I receive half their pay. Now do you mind going and bagging them up for me?"

"That's quite a request," Ludwig said.

"Listen, if we understand each other, then we must help each other," Gustav/Dora said.

"Oh, okay fine. Then I will tell you how you can help me," Ludwig said indignantly.

Ludwig came back with the dead geese and plopped them down next to Gustav/Dora.

"Now, here is how you can help me. I am hosting a banquet at Neuschwanstein. All the guests are there except for two. One I anticipate will be with us soon. The ghost of

Gustav Krupp von Bohlen und Halbach. And the other guest I need is you."

"Me?" Gustav/Dora said surprised. "Why me?"

"This banquet, all the guests are soldiers or people who have committed war crimes. It is time to hold them accountable. I know what all the other guests did. Their priests ,who took refuge in my castle during World War I, enlightened me, but I do not know fully what Gustav Krupp von Bohlen und Halbach did. I knew there would be another war and that he must be judged!"

"How vengeful can you be!" Gustav/Dora said. "I'll help you, but I don't even know your name. What is it?"

The man who had been standing before Gustav/Dora disappeared, and in its place was a swan. Gustav/Dora regained their composure and watched it fly away through their viewfinder, till it was at Neuschwanstein.

***

Back at Neuschwanstein in Singers Hall, the chairs around the oak table were filled, except for one. The ten veterans of the Franco-Prussian War and World War I sat on both sides. The ghost of Gustav Krupp von Bohlen und Halbach sat at one of the heads.

"Sit down Ludwig," the man with the maimed leg said, after Ludwig had landed and come through the window, transforming back into a human. "You must have found the one you love as you were just a swan."

"He found a man," the man with the bandaged head said. "I knew he would. But come Ludwig, sit down at the other head and make this banquet complete. We have waited over fifty years to eat. Don't be rude to your guests."

"I am not the one who is supposed to sit there," Ludwig said quietly.

"Then who is?" all the men except Gustav Krupp von Bohlen und Halbach said in unison.

"Time will tell," Ludwig replied with tears in his eyes.

***

1967

Alfried had been released from prison. Within five years he was the richest man in Europe, and he rebuilt the Krupp firm. Then, the recession hit, banks would no longer lend to him, and he was forced to make a foundation.

"I promised never to make Krupp a stock company, and I have kept my word," the last Krupp said on his death bed.

***

"Ludwig come here! There is someone at the other head of the table. We can finally eat!" the amputee said.

Ludwig rushed in from the library to see Gustav Krupp von Bohlen und Halbach embracing his Alfried, with tears of joy.

"Sit down, sit down. Enough of your mawkish sentimentality," Ludwig bellowed. "Now let's eat!"

The twelve men ate their soup with gusto.

"Well, where is the main course?" Gustav Krupp von Bohlen und Halbach asked.

"There is none," Ludwig replied. "Can't you see there were only two spoons, one for soup and one for dessert.

"Then straight to dessert?" Alfried asked.

"No, gentlemen, I have an alternate course. Ludwig took out a book form behind his back pocket which he had been studying. "Gentlemen who served in the Franco-Prussian War and World War I, behold your deeds."

A misty light emerged from the book, and the ghosts of the victims that had been raped, maimed, and harmed sprung out goosestepping on the table in front of the men. The men's faces became contorted, and they tried to avert their eyes. But they could not—some burst into tears and wailed.

"What is the matter? Too much for you?" Ludwig laughed. Then to the Krupps: "Don't worry your turn will come soon. You can hold each other accountable for what you did. If you do not, you will never leave this castle."

***

Gustav/Dora made the long journey back to Essen with their geese.

"Thanks for the food, we were starving," the foreman said handing the artillery a bag of West-German Marks.

"No keep it," Gustav/Dora said.

"Keep it," the artillery said again. "Give me a spoon instead. The best one you have."

"You got it." The foreman smiled and came back with a golden spoon happy to have his money back. "This spoon is for King Ludwig of Bavaria. Alfried left it in his will to him, go to Neuschwanstein."

Gustav/Dora thanked the foreman and hurried to Neuschwanstein. *Perhaps there still is a seat at the table for me. The man, he is the only one who understands me and what I go through.*

***

When Gustav/Dora entered The Singers Hall, the ghosts of all the victims stopped marching and scurried back into the pages of the book.

"You're just in time!" Ludwig beamed, crossing the hall and hugging Gustav/Dora.

"I wanted to help you, but you disappeared. I brought this." Gustav/Dora held up the golden spoon.

"Oh, excellent!" King Ludwig beamed. "The Krupps are going to need it to eat all their evils. Now tell me, as you know both what their transgressions were. They must have been worse than the ones in the other two wars that Krupp financed. I imagine there is going to be hell to pay!"

Father and son looked at each other with furrowed brows and grasped the table trying to push themselves up. They were stuck.

About the Author

Peter Prizel is an end-of-life care social worker. He recently received his MFA from Manhattanville College. His poetry can be found in magazines and his full-length poetry publications (*Verses of the Soviet Rail*, Cyberwit Publishing) can be found online. He has also recently published two novels: *An Angelic Folly*, and *The Fermented Savior*. Peter lives in the NYC Metropolitan Area with his wife and three daughters. His ten-minute play (*The Note in the Wall*) is slated to be placed on a podcast with Open Door Playhouse this April.

Red Rook Staff

Acquisitions

Olivia LaRose (liaison), Hannah Bazinaw, Lexi Burroughs, Aubrey Case, Caroline Cunningham, Soleil Demars, Charlotte Diel, Jordan Earnest, Malik Erskine, Camryn Haag, Kaira Harper, Angie Henle, Anna Luis, Kalyn King, Addison Lusco, Ainslee Monroe, Ava Rudd, Elle Sims, Scarlet Sodergren, Kiley Stevens, Alyssa Walker, Tatum Walker, Alyssa Wallner

Audio

McKenzie Knight (liaison), Elanor Asuncion-Crabb, Soleil Demars, Andrea Gonzalez Larregoity, Izzy Novak, Tatum Walker

Design

DeAndra Gauntt (liaison), Anna Cobb, MiKayla Davis, Alexandria Gauntt, Elizabeth Golembiewski, Ainsley Greer, Andrew Kelley, Anna Luis, Anna White

Promotions

Maya Mungo (liaison), Jackson Davidson, Camryn Haag, Kaira Harper, Sarah Vance Harrison, Kalyn King, Dante Larkins, Ella Lybarger, Hannah Mauck, Lex Mroczko, Averi O'Brien, Karmen Paige

Prose Editing

Jack Armstrong (liaison), Camryn Haag (liaison), Victoria Bell, Henry Bowles, Aubrey Case, MiKayla Davis, Soleil Demars, Charlotte Diel, Aaron Hightower, Livi King, Dante Larkins, Olivia LaRose, Anna Luis, Ainslee Monroe, Jillian Naylor, Scarlet Sodergren, Jaxiel Tavarez, Alyssa Wallner

Website

Ansel Smith (liaison), Henry Bowles, Swastee Regmi, Luke Theobald

Special Projects

Wrenley Brown, Livi King, Karmen Paige

Faculty Advisers

Paul Albano, Sarah Cheshire, Merrill Lee Girardeau, Stephanie Marker, Jane Morton

About the Press

Red Rook Press is an award-winning, student-run publishing house from the University of Alabama. Our goal is to foster and promote the creative minds of undergraduate and graduate students still establishing themselves in the writing world by giving them the opportunity to bring their voice to life. With our staff of dedicated undergraduates student-editors and professional advisors, we bring several new books of prose and poetry into the world every academic year.

Find us at redrookpress.org